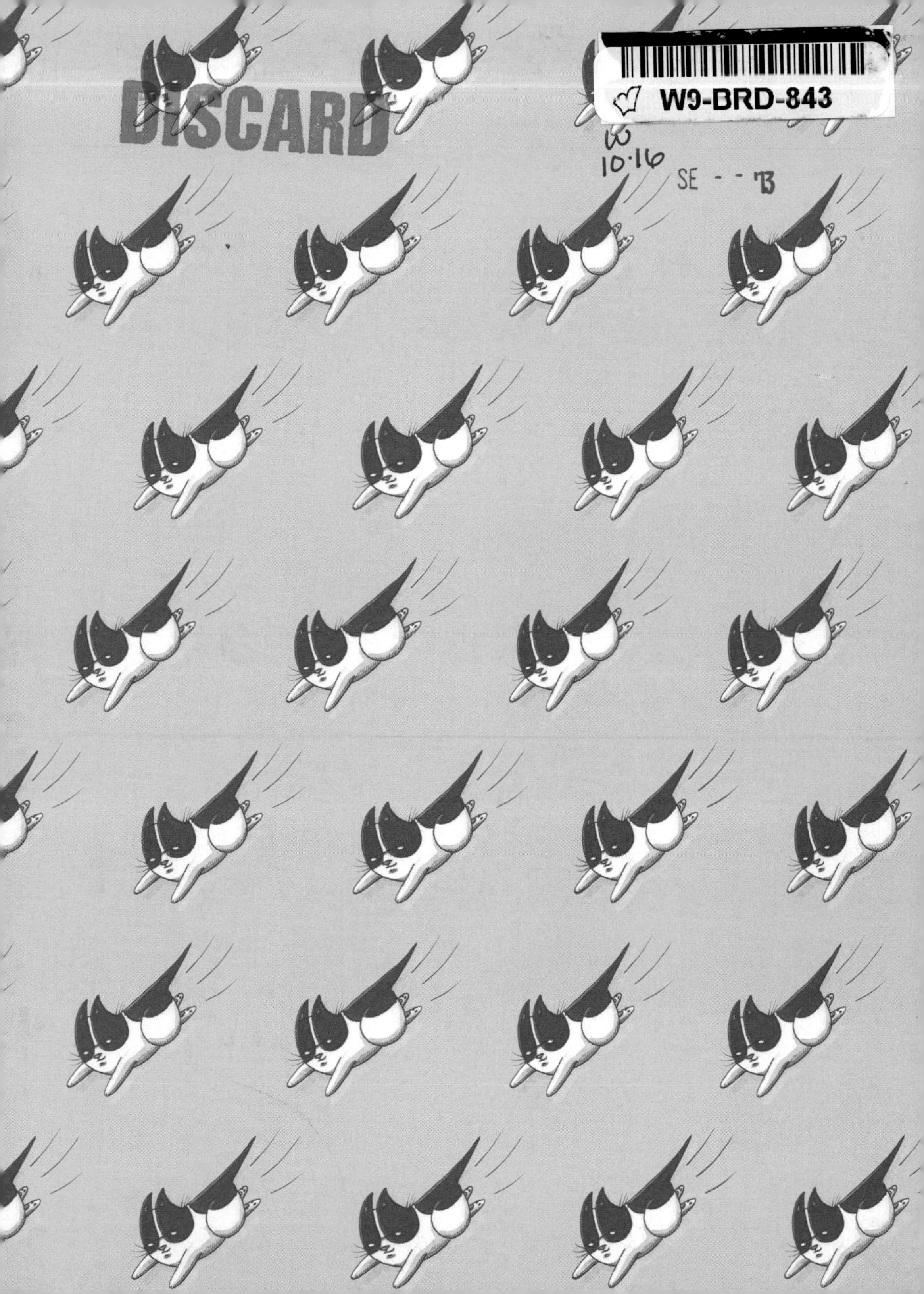

BINKY

LICENSE TO SCRATCH

KIDS CAN PRESS

To Malcolm and Neala, for always rooting for Binky

Text and illustrations © 2013 Ashley Spires

Kids Can Press acknowledges the financial support of the Government of Ontario, through the Ontario Media Development Corporation's Ontario Book Initiative; the Ontario Arts Council; the Canada Council for the Arts; and the Government of Canada, through the CBF, for our publishing activity.

Published in Canada by
Kids Can Press Ltd.
25 Dockside Drive
Toronto, ON M5A 0B5

Published in the U.S. by
Kids Can Press Ltd.
2250 Military Road
Tonawanda, NY 14150

www.kidscanpress.com

The artwork in this book was rendered in ink, watercolor, cat fur, bits of kitty litter, the occasional paw print, dog slobber and some biological matter we cannot name.
The text is set in Fontoon.

Edited by Karen Li and Yasemin Uçar
Designed by Julia Naimska
Series design by Karen Powers

The hardcover edition of this book is smyth sewn casebound.
The paperback edition of this book is limp sewn with a drawn-on cover.
Manufactured in Shen Zhen, Guang Dong, P.R. China, in 4/2013 by Printplus Limited.

CM 13 0 9 8 7 6 5 4 3 2 1
CM PA 13 0 9 8 7 6 5 4 3 2 1

Library and Archives Canada Cataloguing in Publication

Spires, Ashley, 1978–
Binky, license to scratch / written and illustrated by Ashley Spires.

(A Binky adventure)
ISBN 978-1-55453-963-5 (bound)   ISBN 978-1-55453-964-2 (pbk.)

I. Title. II. Series: Spires, Ashley, 1978–. Binky adventure.

PS8637.P57B545 2013   jC813'.6   C2012-908580-4

Kids Can Press is a *Corus*™ Entertainment company

NO ANIMALS WERE HARMED IN THE MAKING OF THIS BOOK. A CAT HAD SOME ROUTINE BLOODWORK DONE AND A DOG WAS SUBJECTED TO SOME FOUL-TASTING LEFTOVERS, BUT THAT WAS THE EXTENT OF IT.

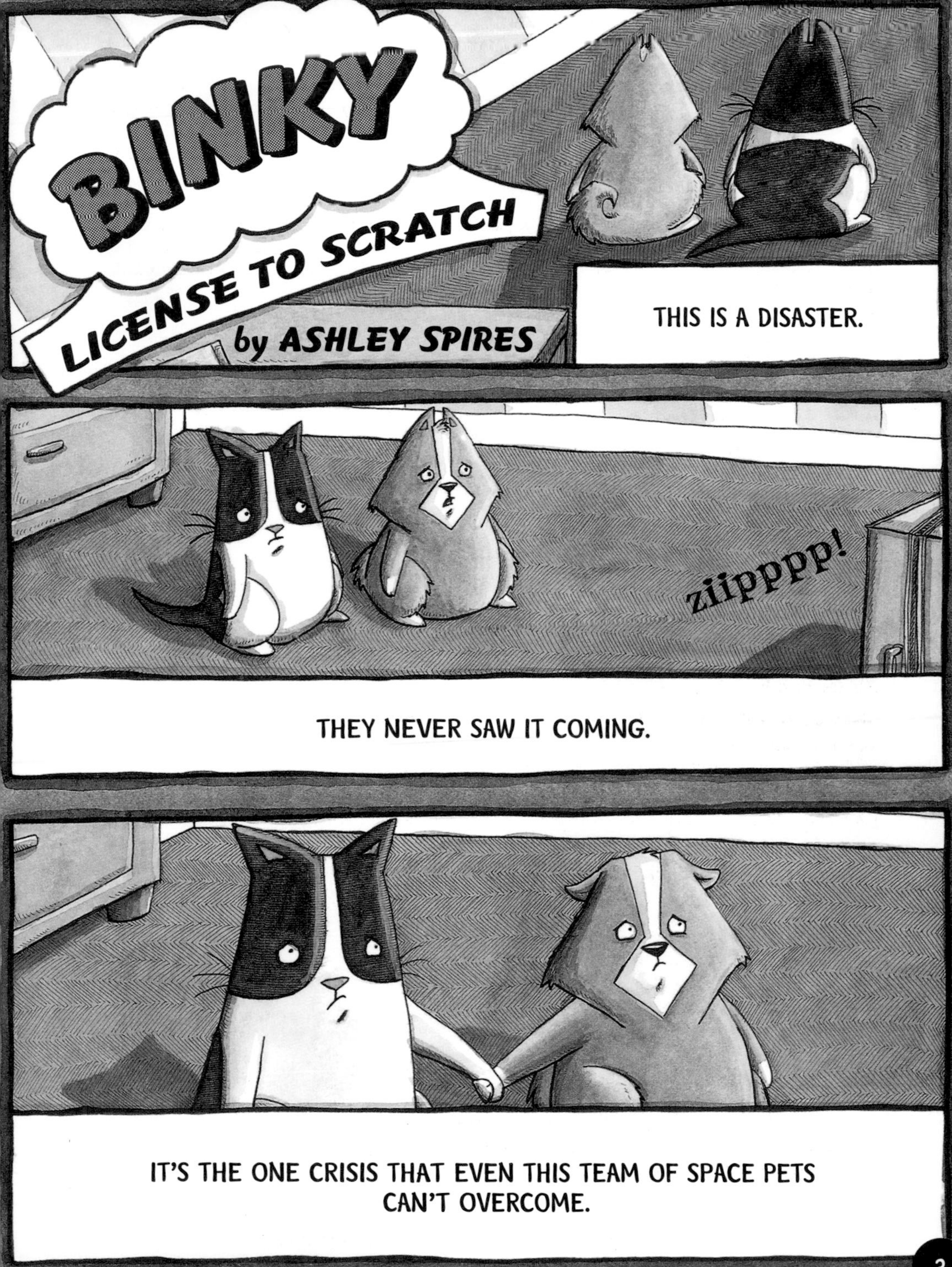

BINKY
LICENSE TO SCRATCH
by ASHLEY SPIRES
THIS IS A DISASTER.
ziipppp!
THEY NEVER SAW IT COMING.
IT'S THE ONE CRISIS THAT EVEN THIS TEAM OF SPACE PETS CAN'T OVERCOME.

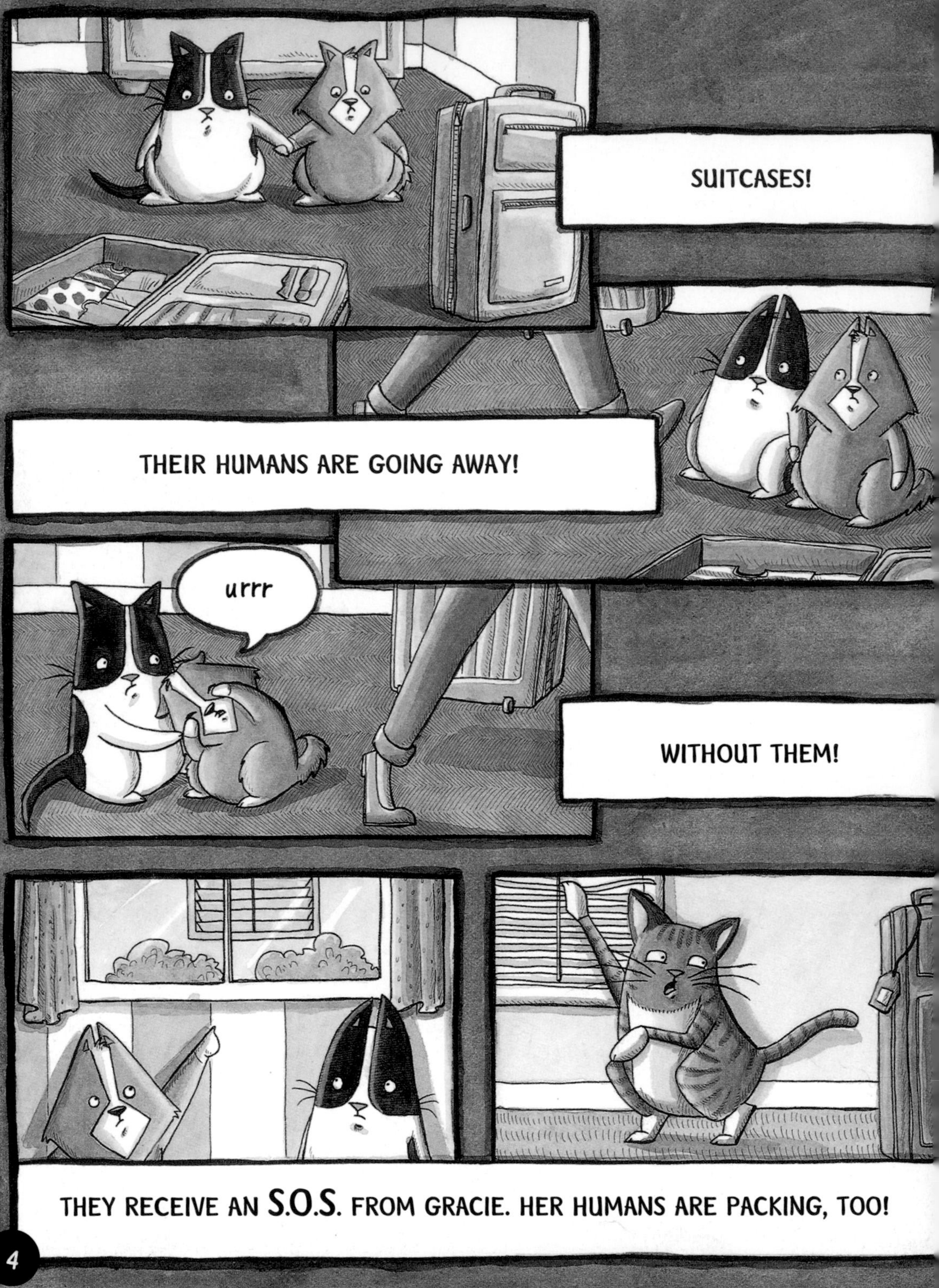

SUITCASES!
THEIR HUMANS ARE GOING AWAY!
urrr
WITHOUT THEM!
THEY RECEIVE AN S.O.S. FROM GRACIE. HER HUMANS ARE PACKING, TOO!

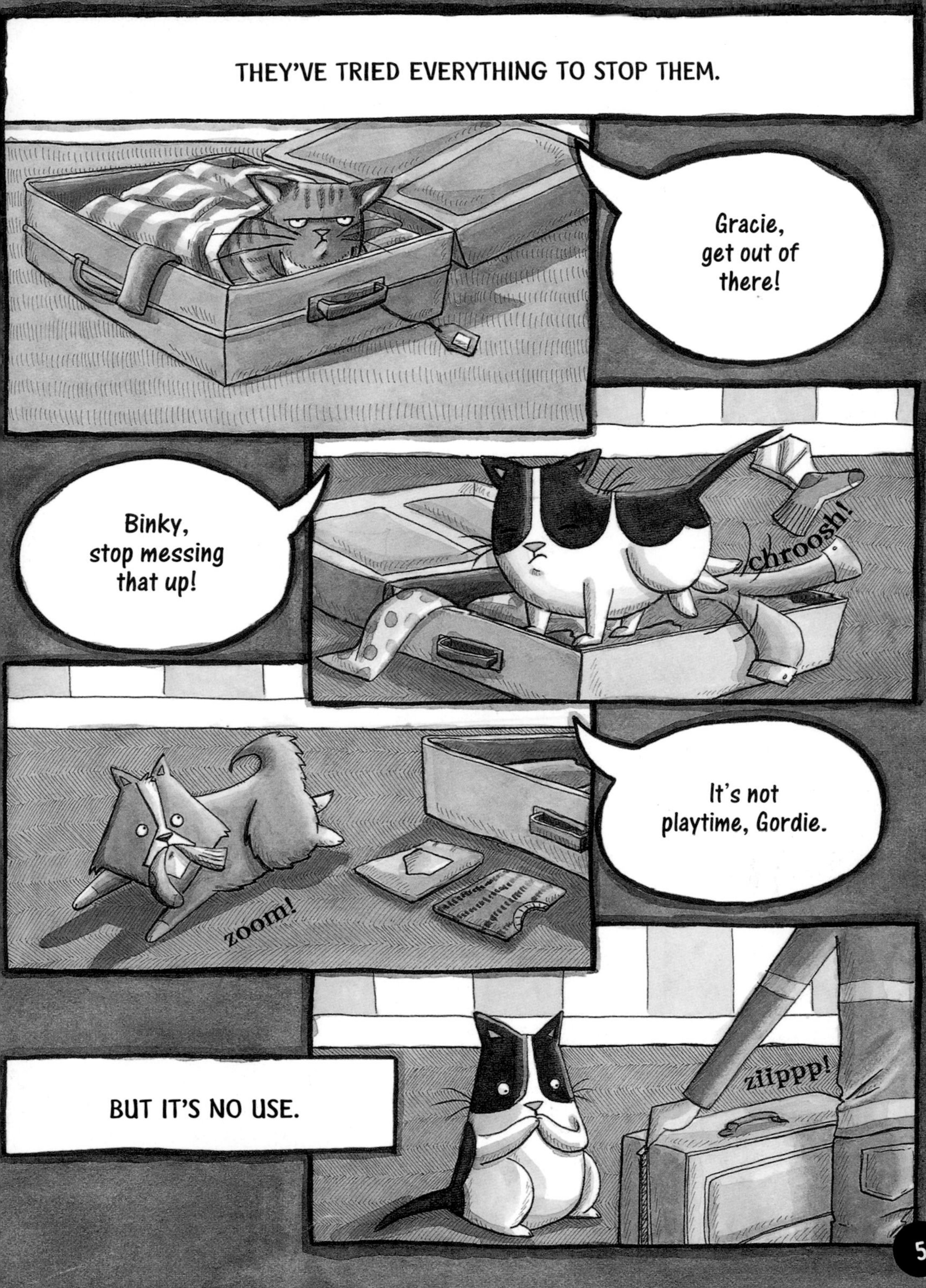
THEY'VE TRIED EVERYTHING TO STOP THEM.
Gracie, get out of there!
Binky, stop messing that up!
chroosh!
It's not playtime, Gordie.
zoom!
BUT IT'S NO USE.
ziippp!

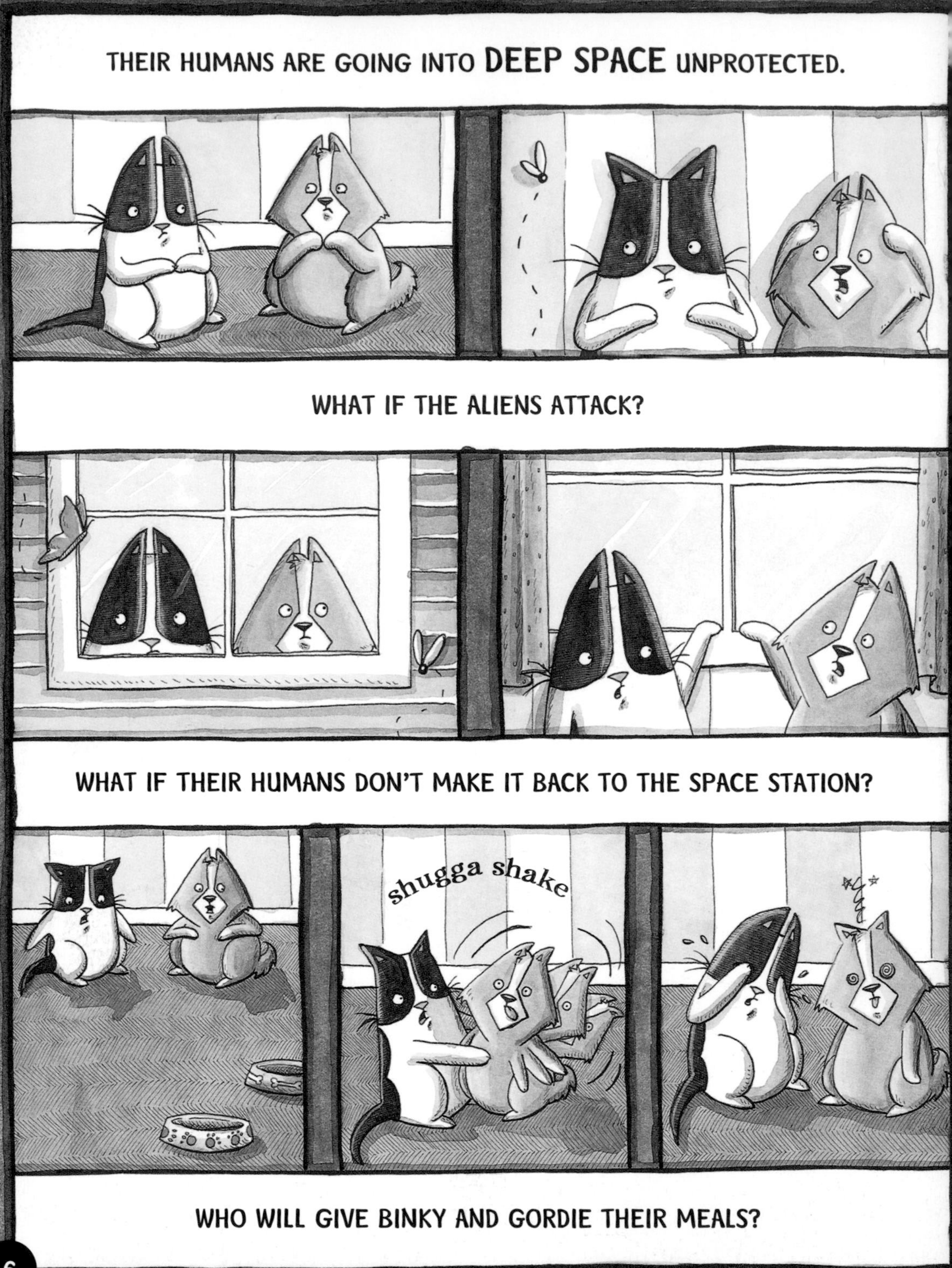
THEIR HUMANS ARE GOING INTO DEEP SPACE UNPROTECTED.
WHAT IF THE ALIENS ATTACK?
WHAT IF THEIR HUMANS DON'T MAKE IT BACK TO THE SPACE STATION?
shugga shake
WHO WILL GIVE BINKY AND GORDIE THEIR MEALS?

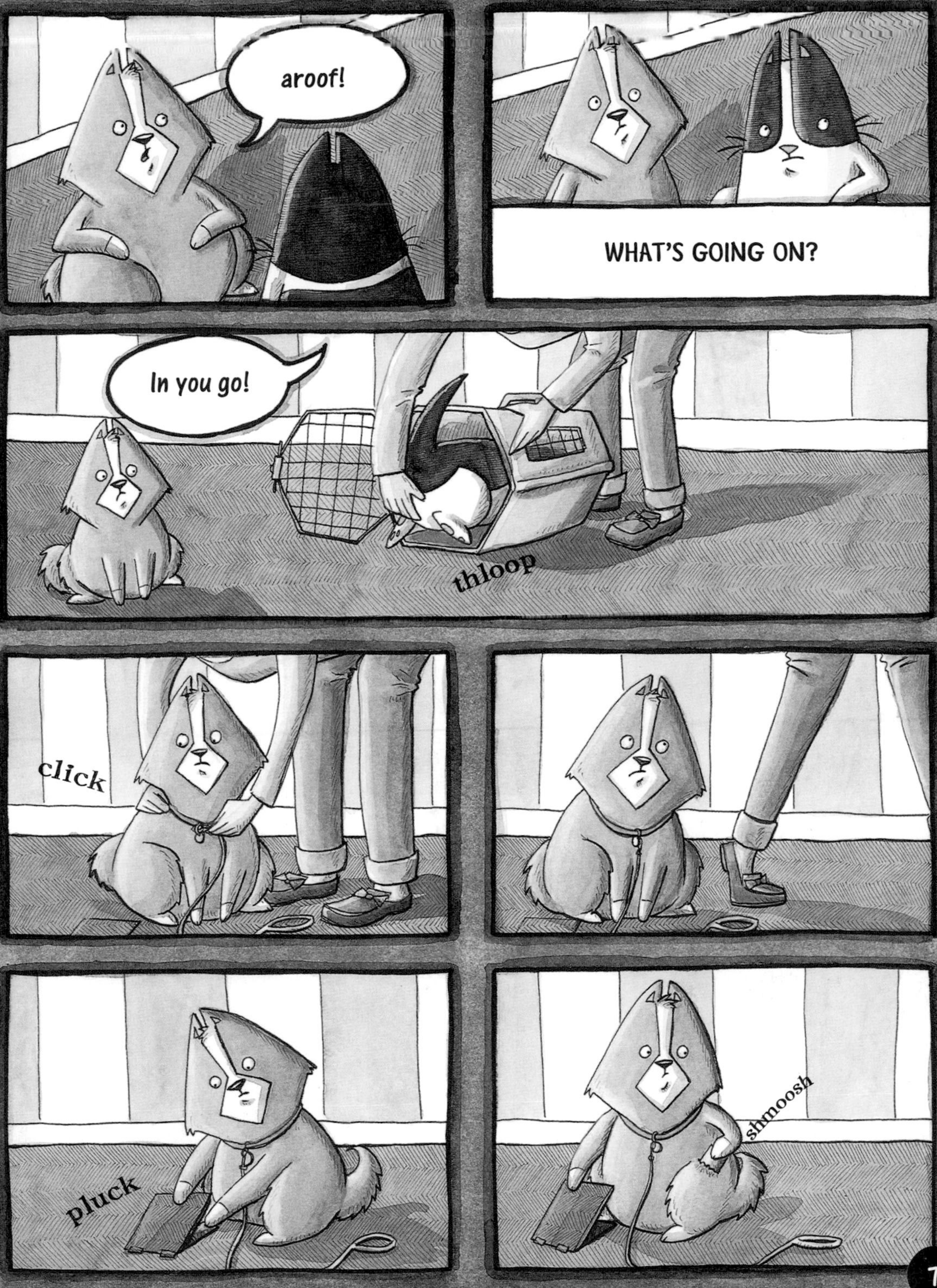
aroof!
WHAT'S GOING ON?
In you go!
thloop
click
pluck
shmoosh

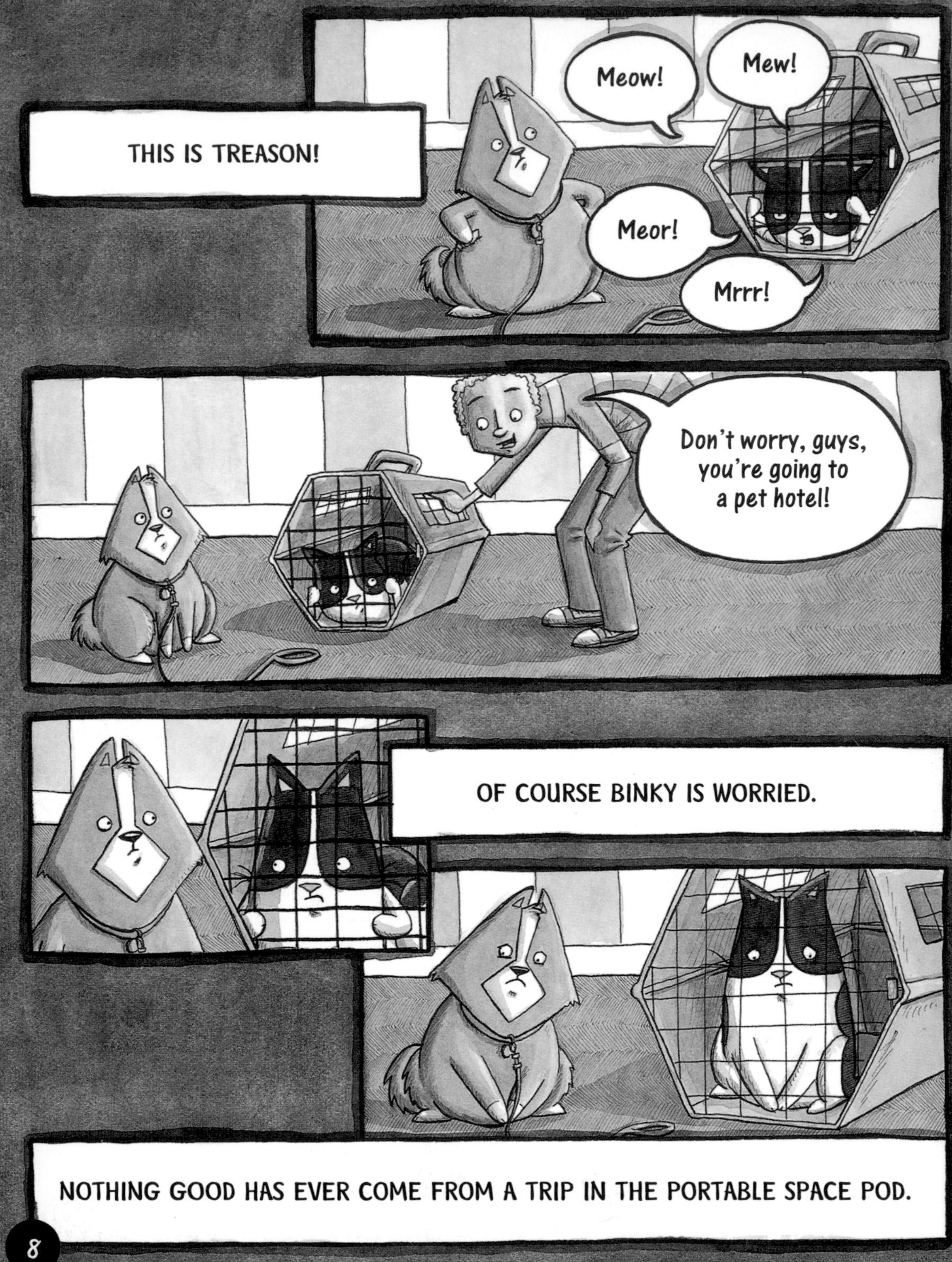
THIS IS TREASON!
Meow!
Mew!
Meor!
Mrrr!
Don't worry, guys, you're going to a pet hotel!
OF COURSE BINKY IS WORRIED.
NOTHING GOOD HAS EVER COME FROM A TRIP IN THE PORTABLE SPACE POD.

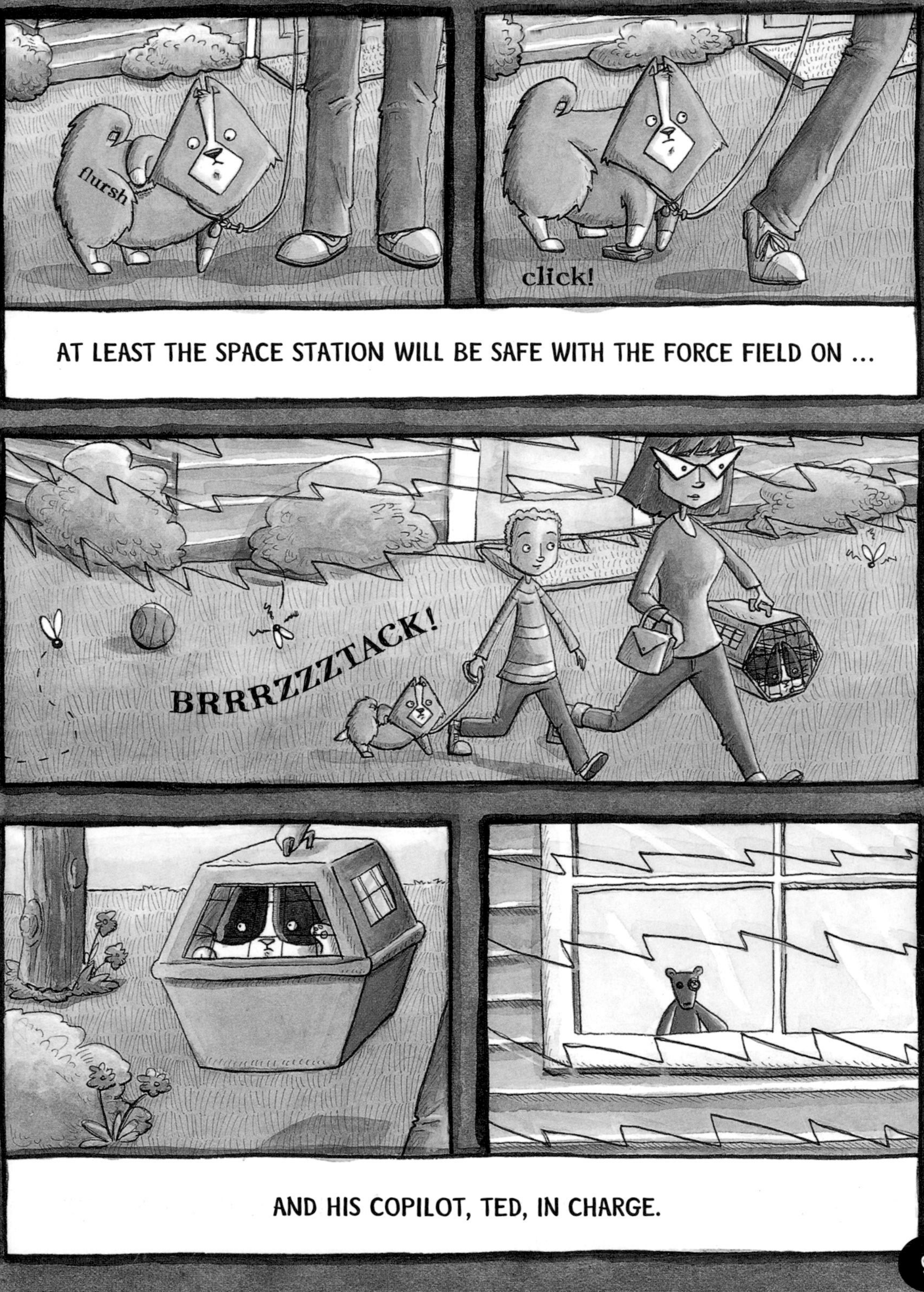
flursh
click!
AT LEAST THE SPACE STATION WILL BE SAFE WITH THE FORCE FIELD ON ...
BRRRZZZTACK!
AND HIS COPILOT, TED, IN CHARGE.

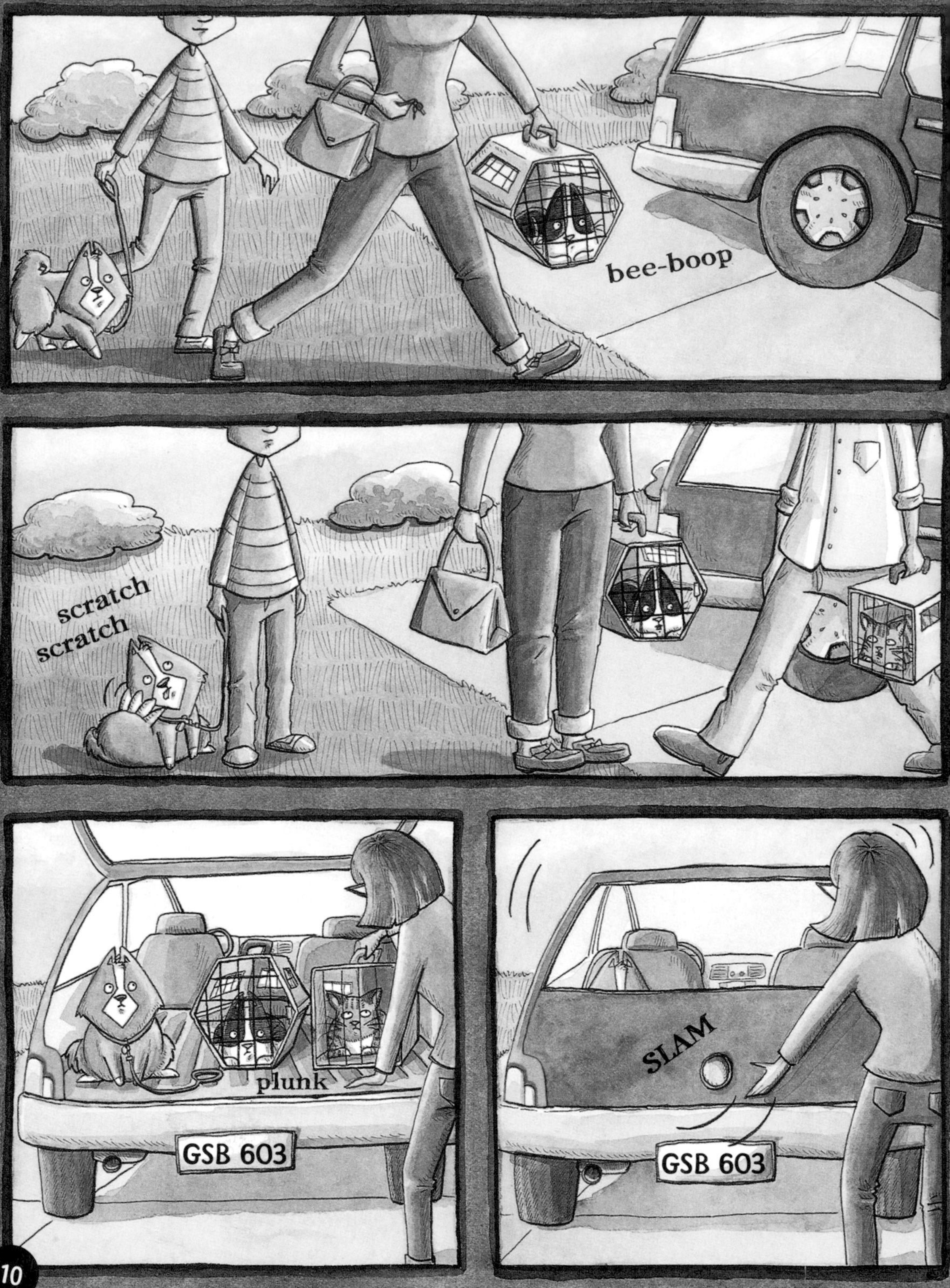
bee-boop
scratch
scratch
plunk
GSB 603
SLAM
GSB 603

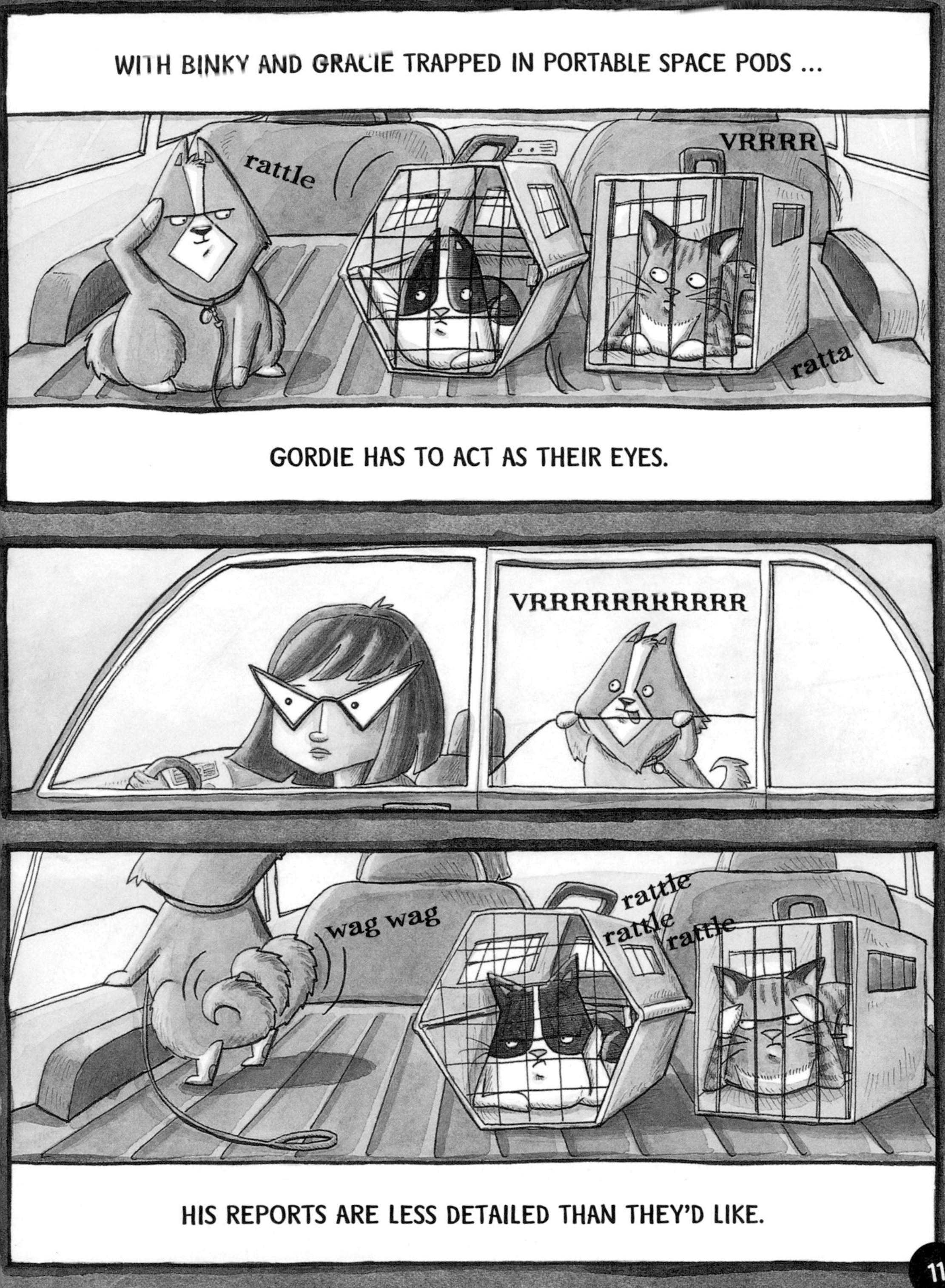
WITH BINKY AND GRACIE TRAPPED IN PORTABLE SPACE PODS ...
rattle
VRRRR
ratta
GORDIE HAS TO ACT AS THEIR EYES.
VRRRRRRRRRRR
wag wag
rattle
rattle
rattle
HIS REPORTS ARE LESS DETAILED THAN THEY'D LIKE.

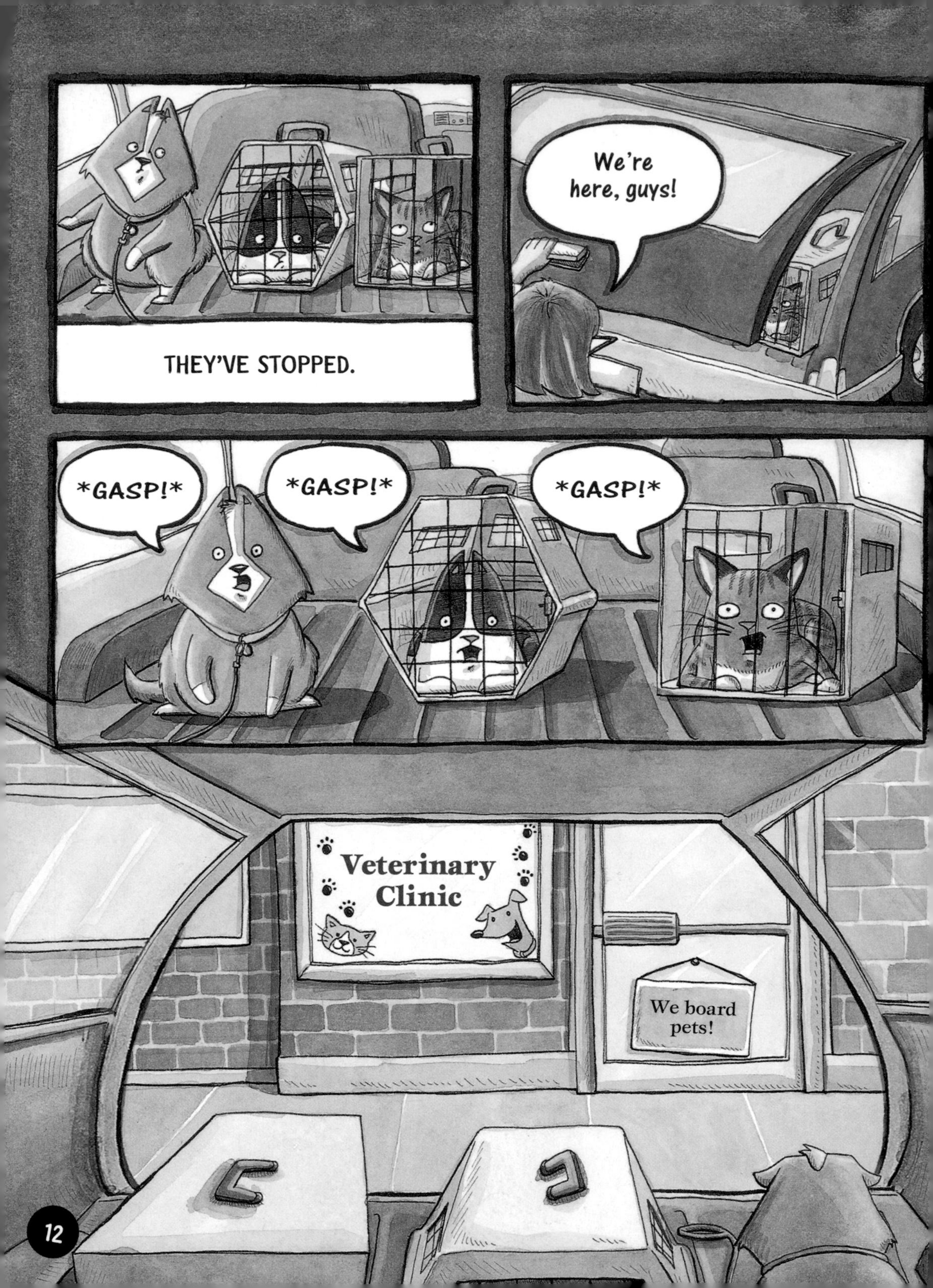
THEY'VE STOPPED.
We're here, guys!
GASP!
GASP!
GASP!
Veterinary Clinic
We board pets!

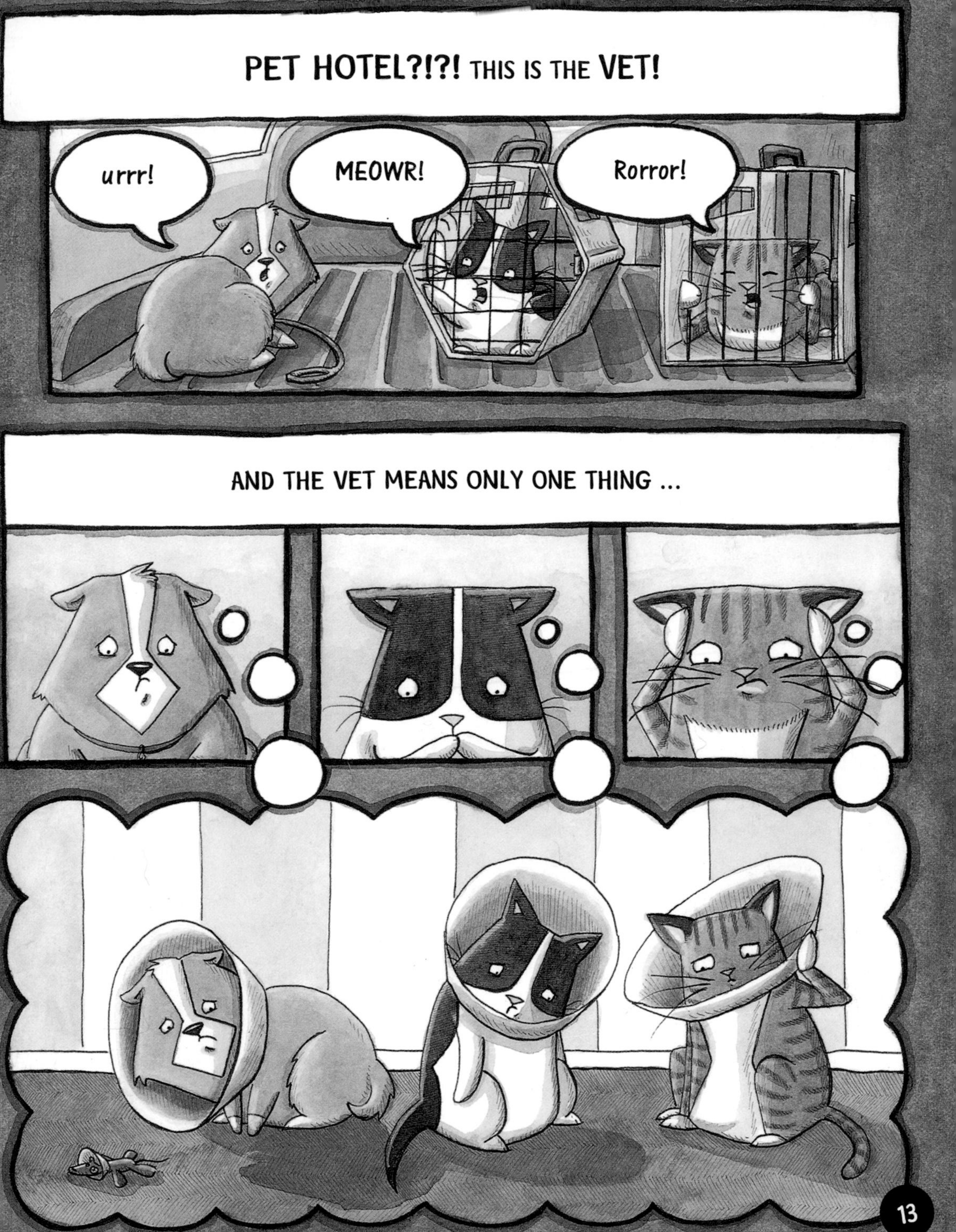
PET HOTEL?!?! THIS IS THE VET!
urrr!
MEOWR!
Rorror!
AND THE VET MEANS ONLY ONE THING ...

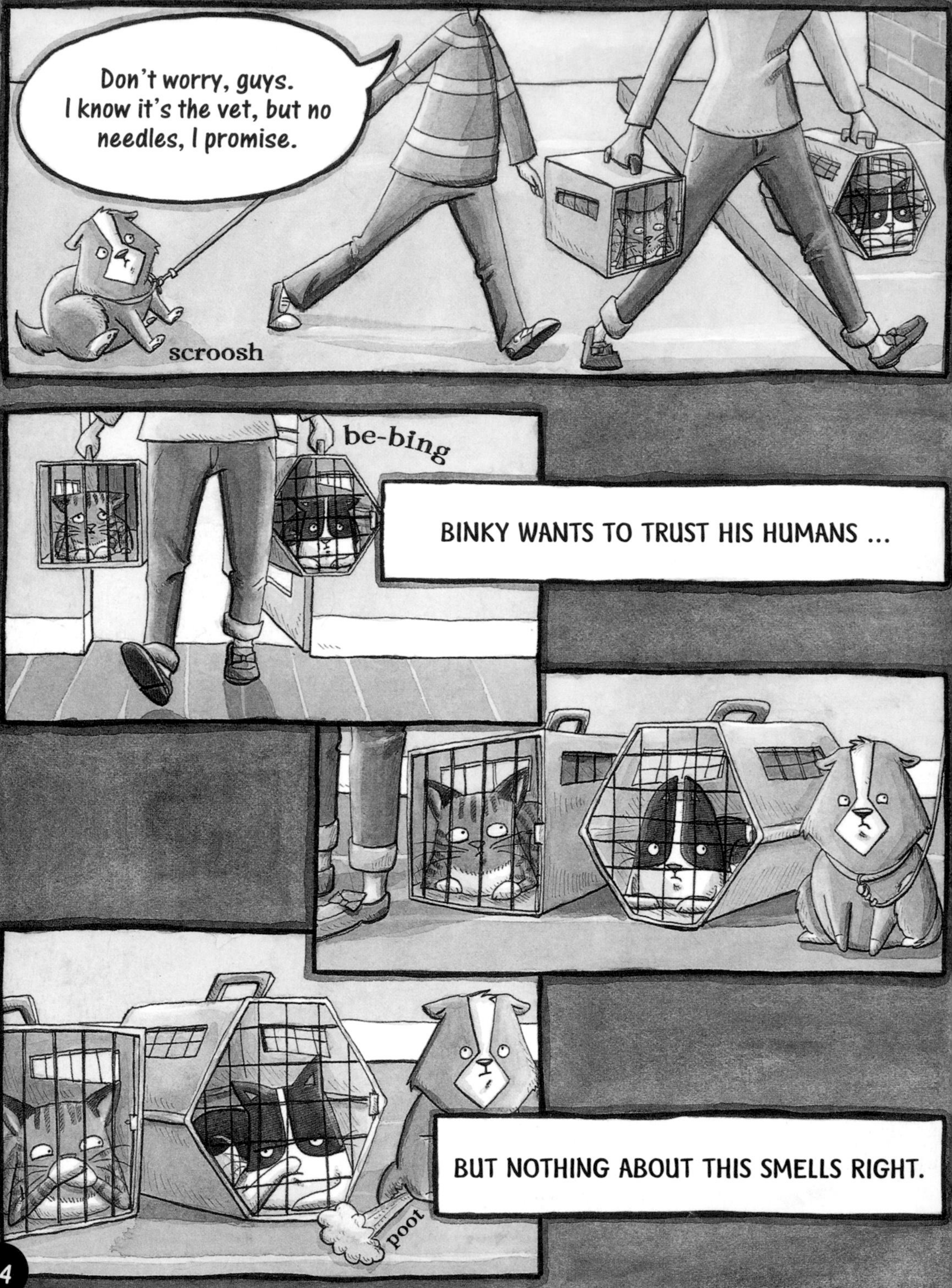
Don't worry, guys.
I know it's the vet, but no
needles, I promise.
scroosh
be-bing
BINKY WANTS TO TRUST HIS HUMANS ...
BUT NOTHING ABOUT THIS SMELLS RIGHT.
poot

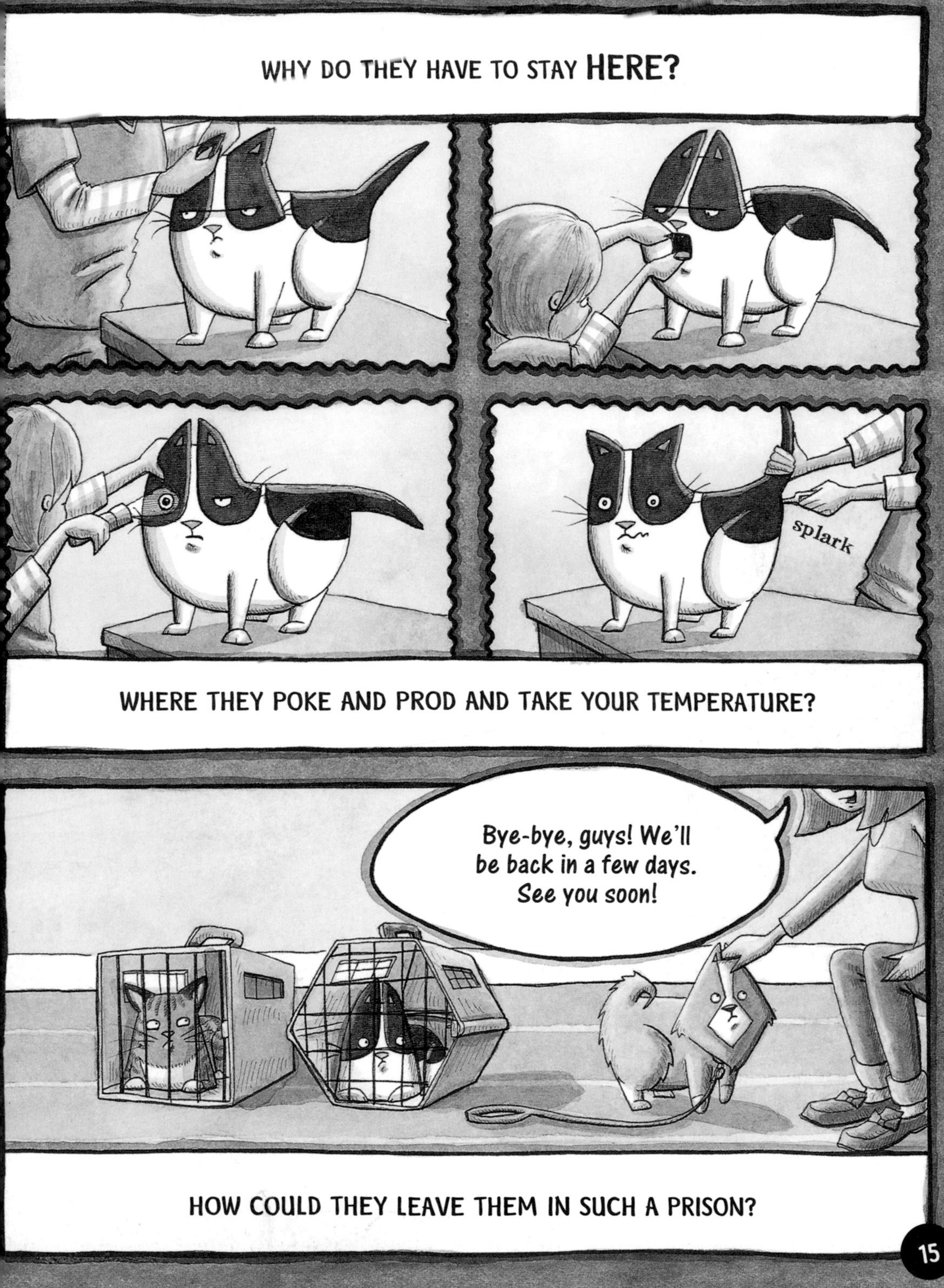
WHY DO THEY HAVE TO STAY HERE?
splark
WHERE THEY POKE AND PROD AND TAKE YOUR TEMPERATURE?
Bye-bye, guys! We'll be back in a few days. See you soon!
HOW COULD THEY LEAVE THEM IN SUCH A PRISON?

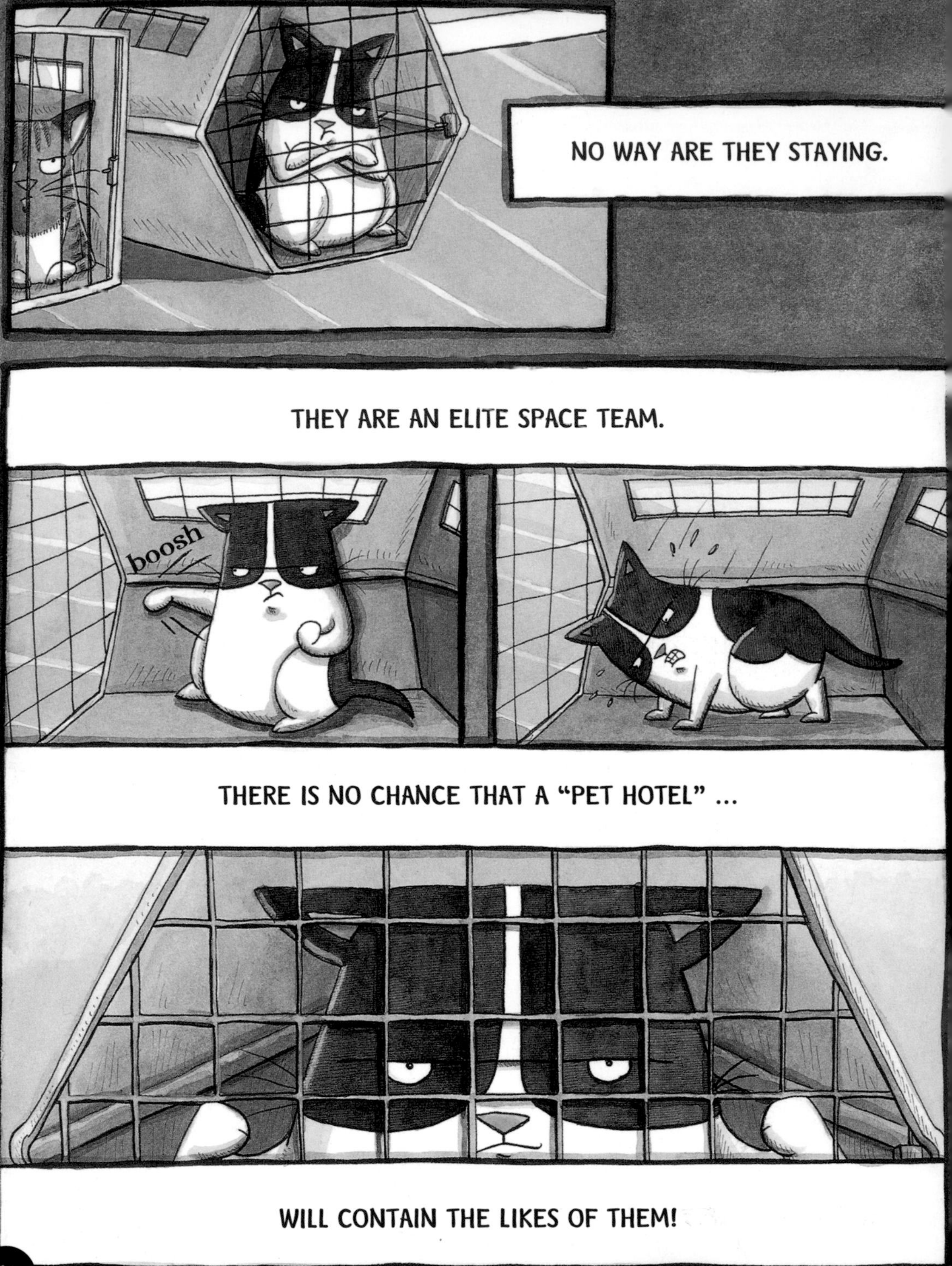
NO WAY ARE THEY STAYING.
THEY ARE AN ELITE SPACE TEAM.
boosh
THERE IS NO CHANCE THAT A "PET HOTEL" ...
WILL CONTAIN THE LIKES OF THEM!

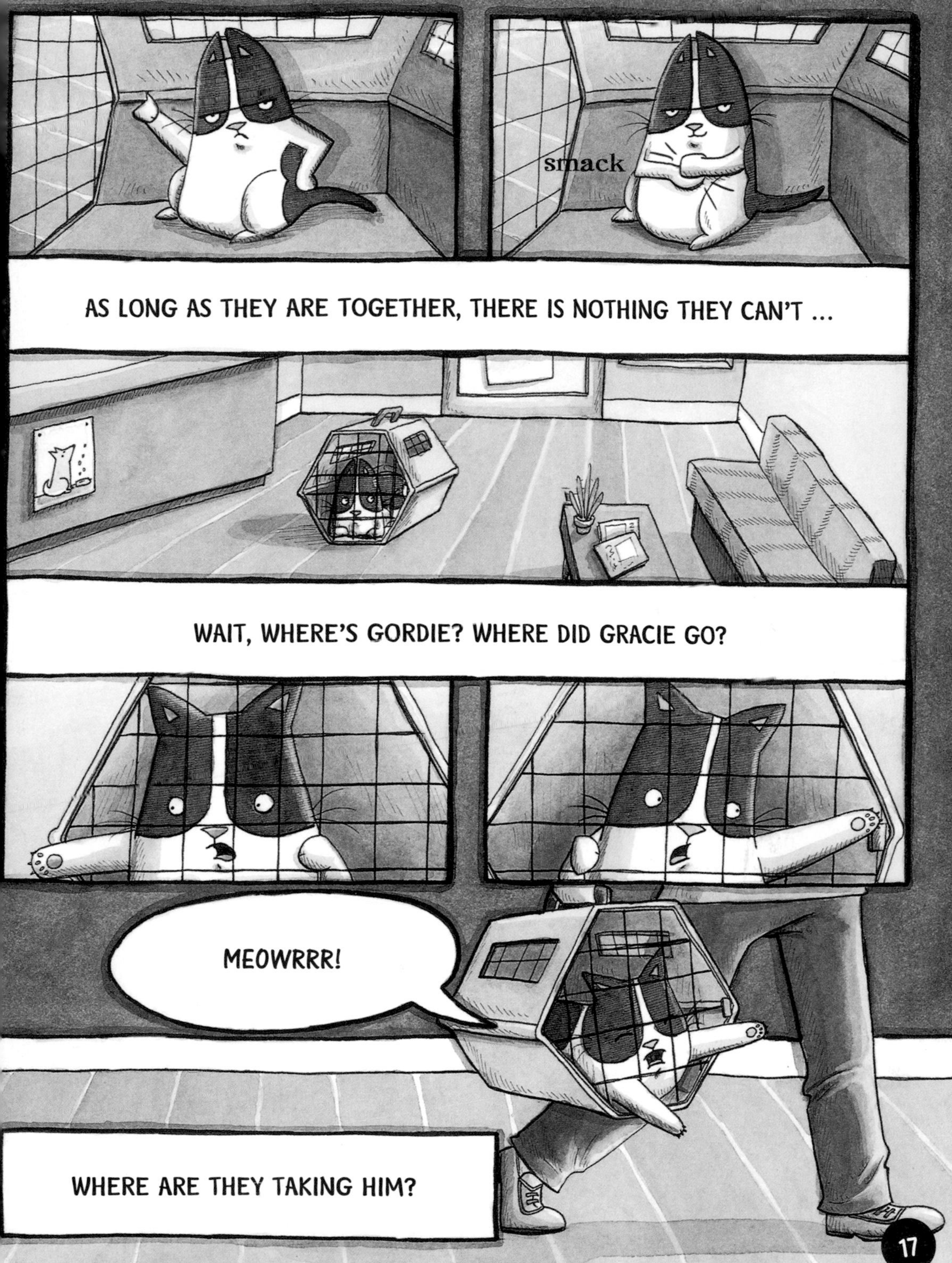
smack
AS LONG AS THEY ARE TOGETHER, THERE IS NOTHING THEY CAN'T ...
WAIT, WHERE'S GORDIE? WHERE DID GRACIE GO?
MEOWRRR!
WHERE ARE THEY TAKING HIM?

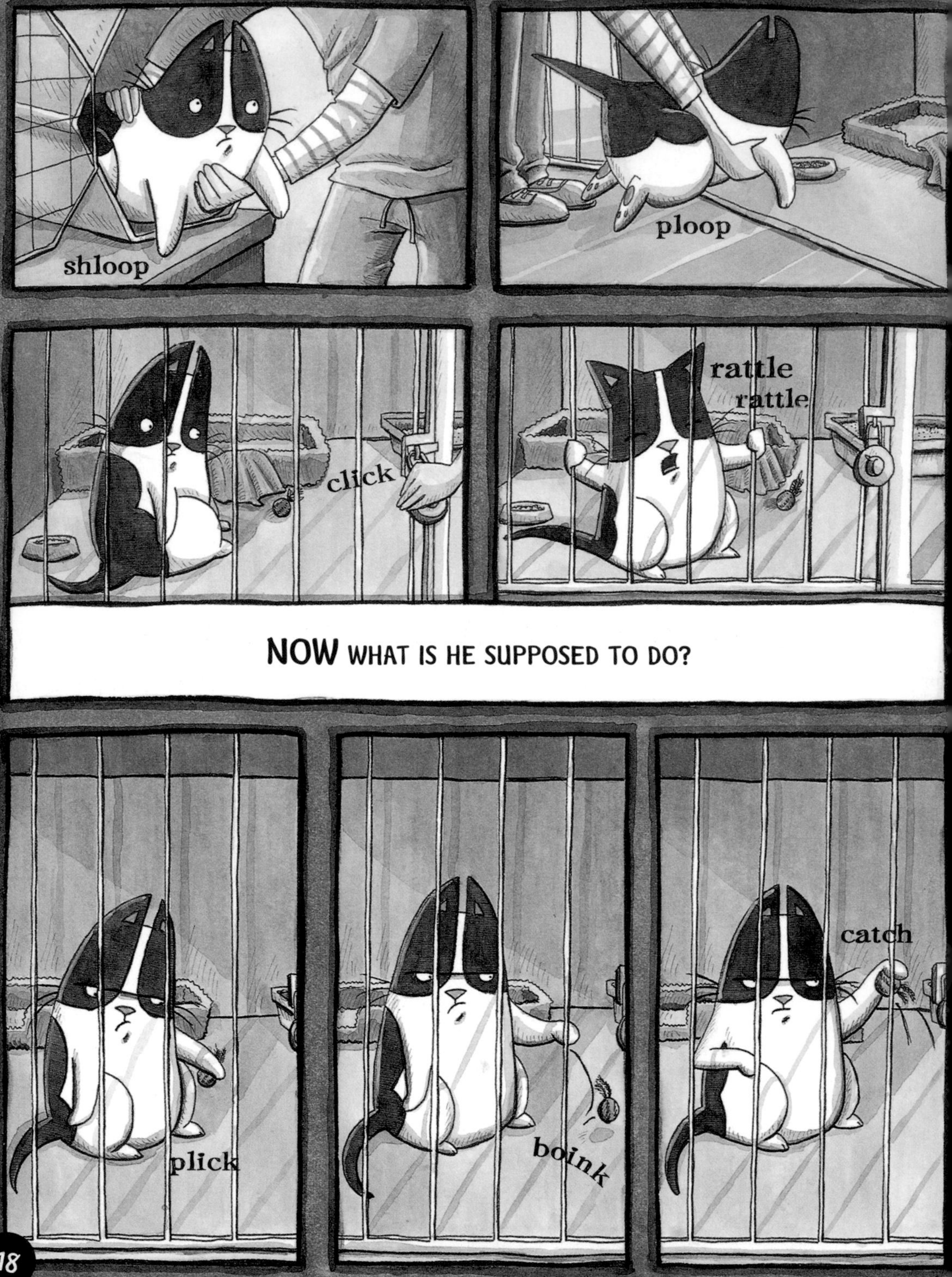
shloop
ploop
click
rattle
rattle
NOW WHAT IS HE SUPPOSED TO DO?
plick
boink
catch

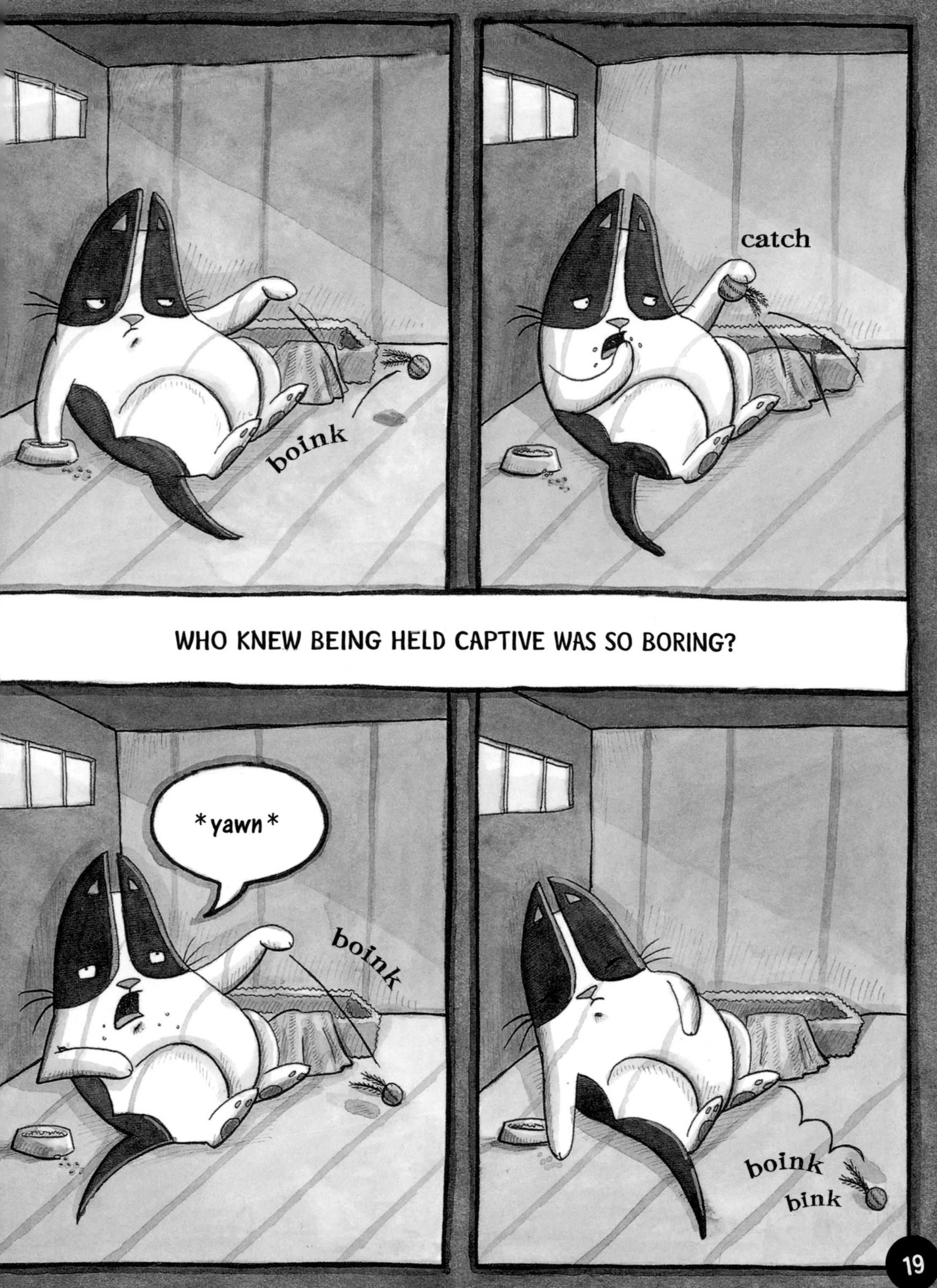
boink
catch
WHO KNEW BEING HELD CAPTIVE WAS SO BORING?
yawn
boink
boink
bink

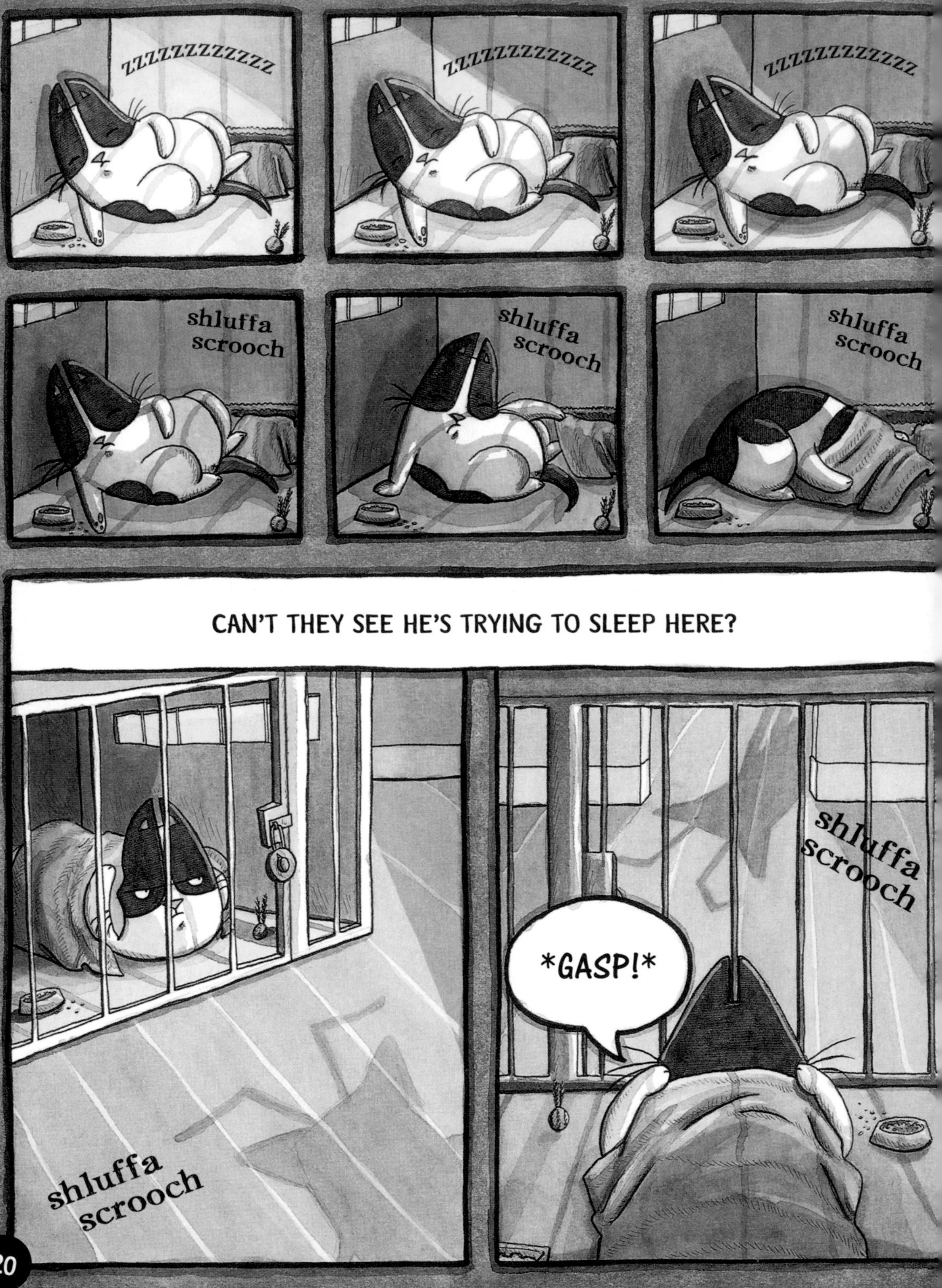
zzzzzzzzzzz
zzzzzzzzzzz
zzzzzzzzzzz
shluffa scrooch
shluffa scrooch
shluffa scrooch
CAN'T THEY SEE HE'S TRYING TO SLEEP HERE?
shluffa scrooch
shluffa scrooch
GASP!

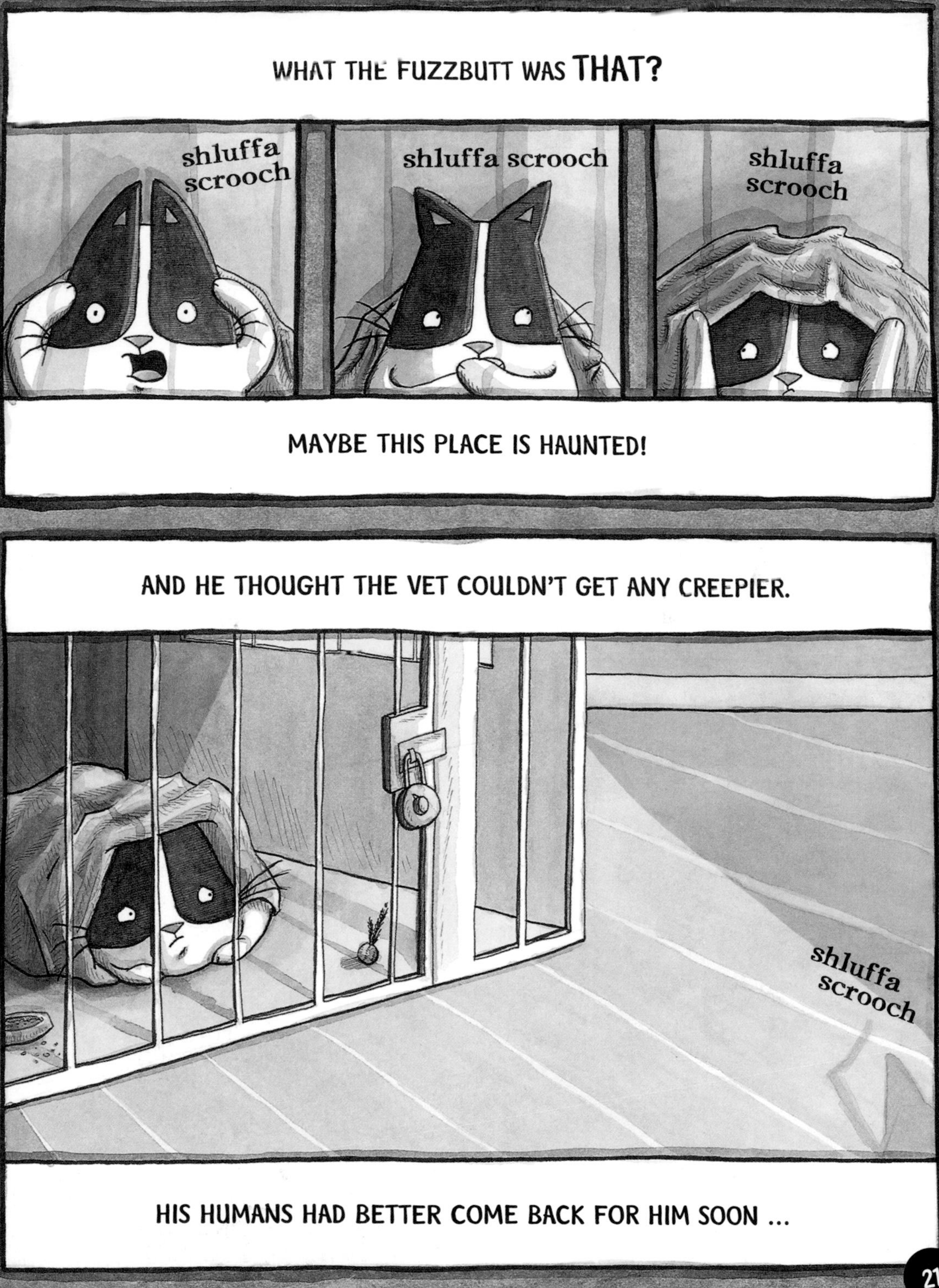
WHAT THE FUZZBUTT WAS THAT?
shluffa scrooch
shluffa scrooch
shluffa scrooch
MAYBE THIS PLACE IS HAUNTED!
AND HE THOUGHT THE VET COULDN'T GET ANY CREEPIER.
shluffa scrooch
HIS HUMANS HAD BETTER COME BACK FOR HIM SOON ...

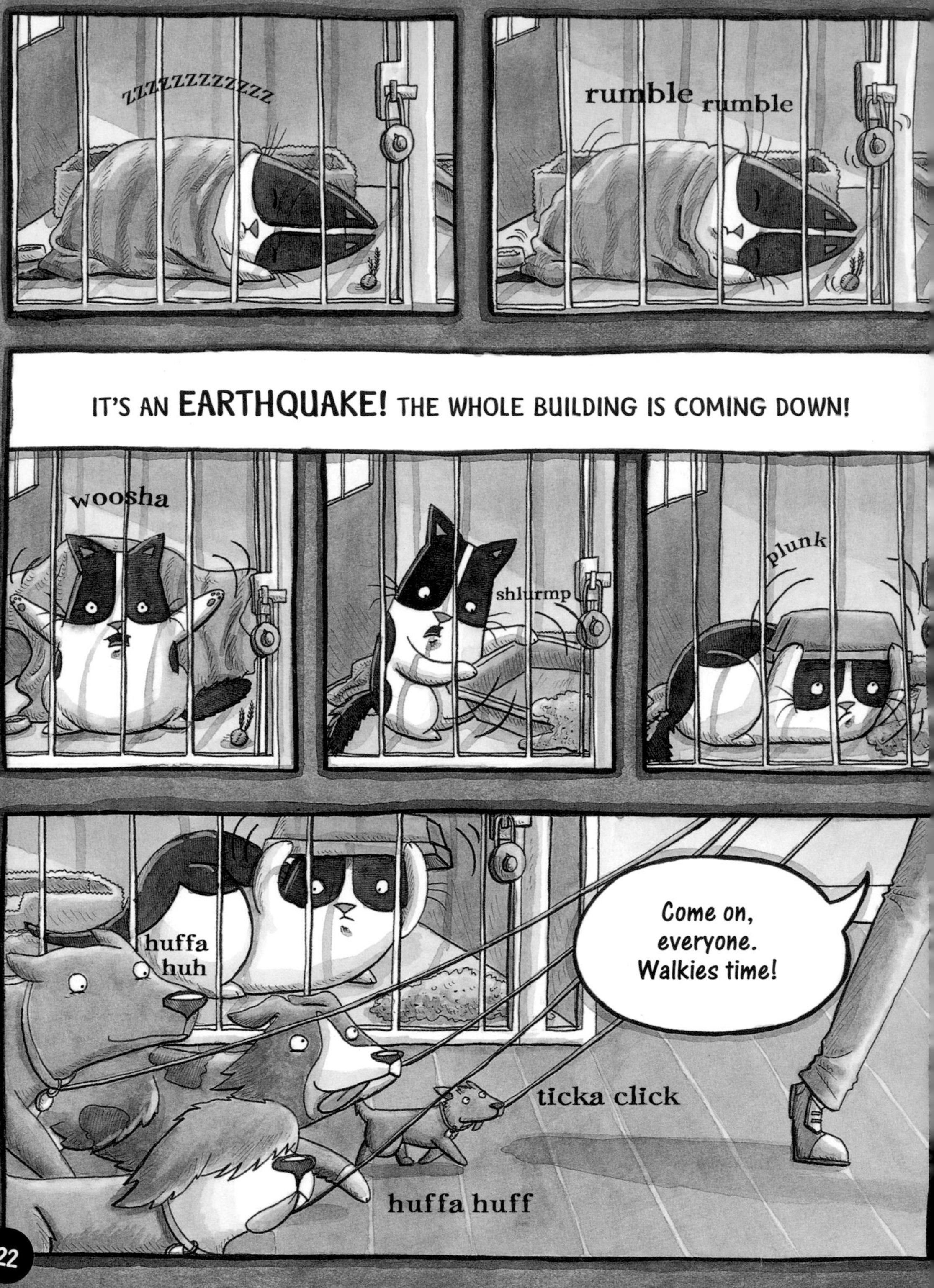
zzzzzzzzzzz
rumble rumble
IT'S AN EARTHQUAKE! THE WHOLE BUILDING IS COMING DOWN!
woosha
shlurmp
plunk
huffa huh
Come on, everyone. Walkies time!
ticka click
huffa huff

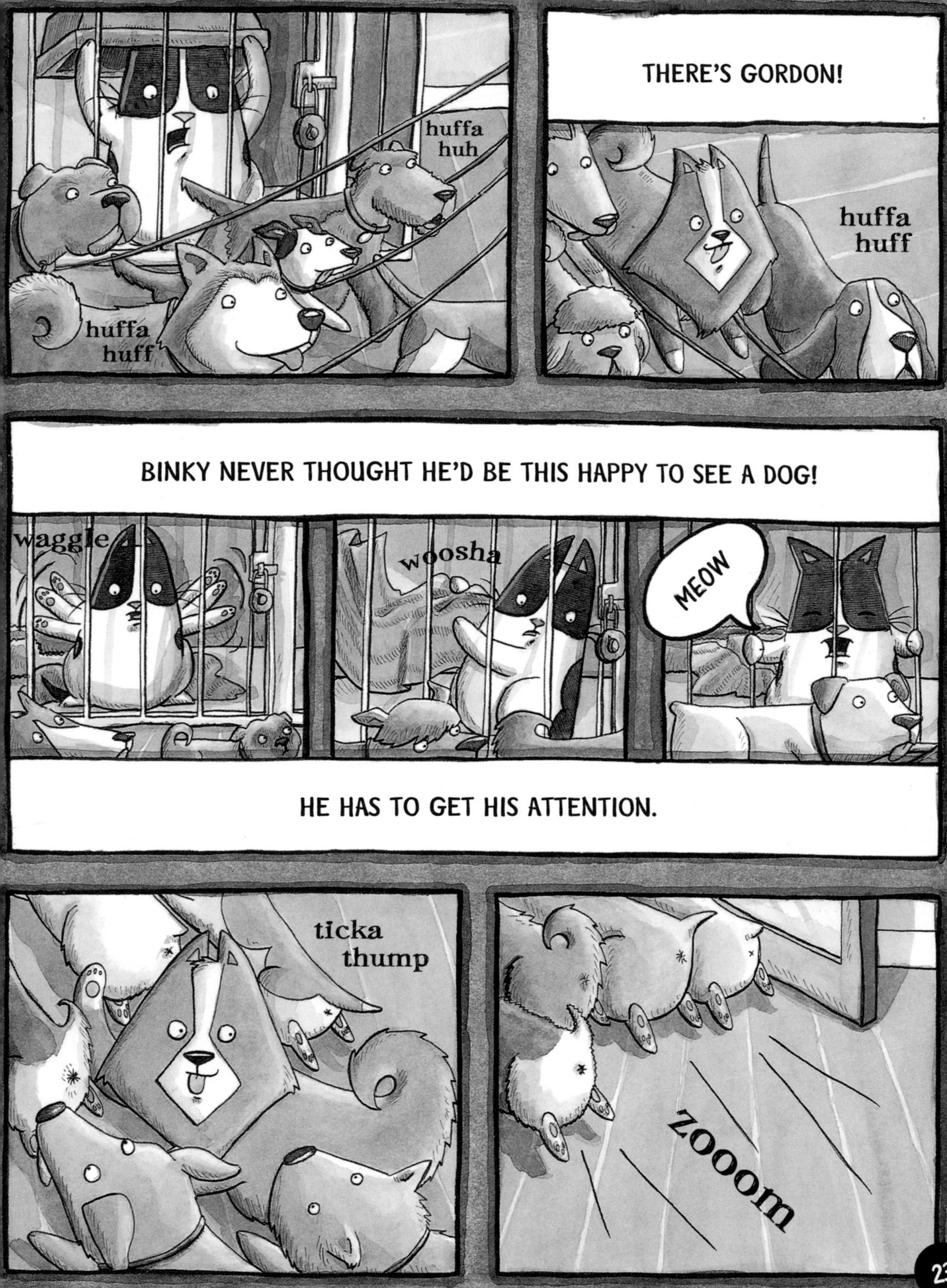
huffa
huh
huffa
huff
THERE'S GORDON!
huffa
huff
BINKY NEVER THOUGHT HE'D BE THIS HAPPY TO SEE A DOG!
waggle
woosha
MEOW
HE HAS TO GET HIS ATTENTION.
ticka
thump
zooom

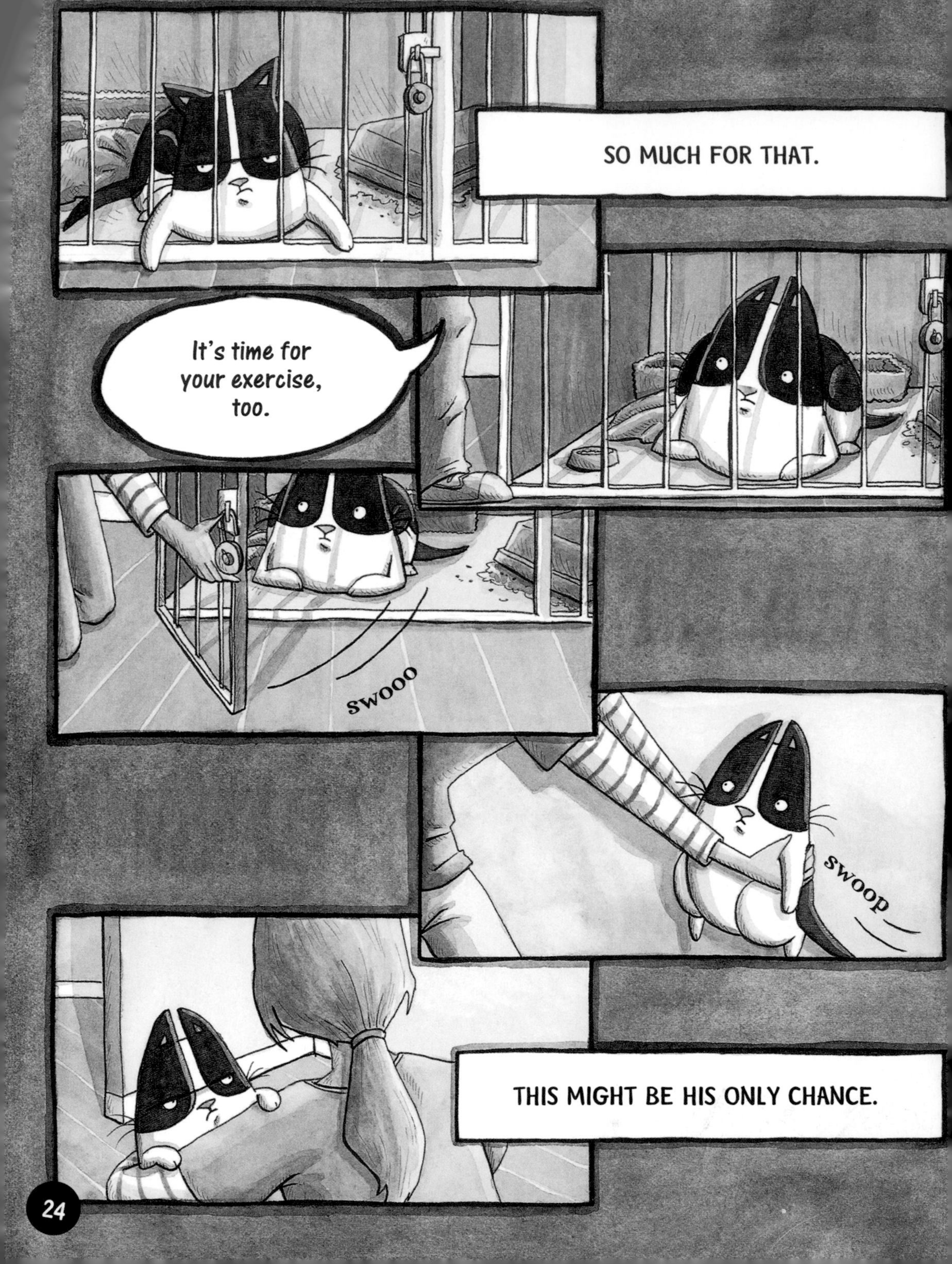
SO MUCH FOR THAT.
It's time for your exercise, too.
SWOOO
SWOOP
THIS MIGHT BE HIS ONLY CHANCE.

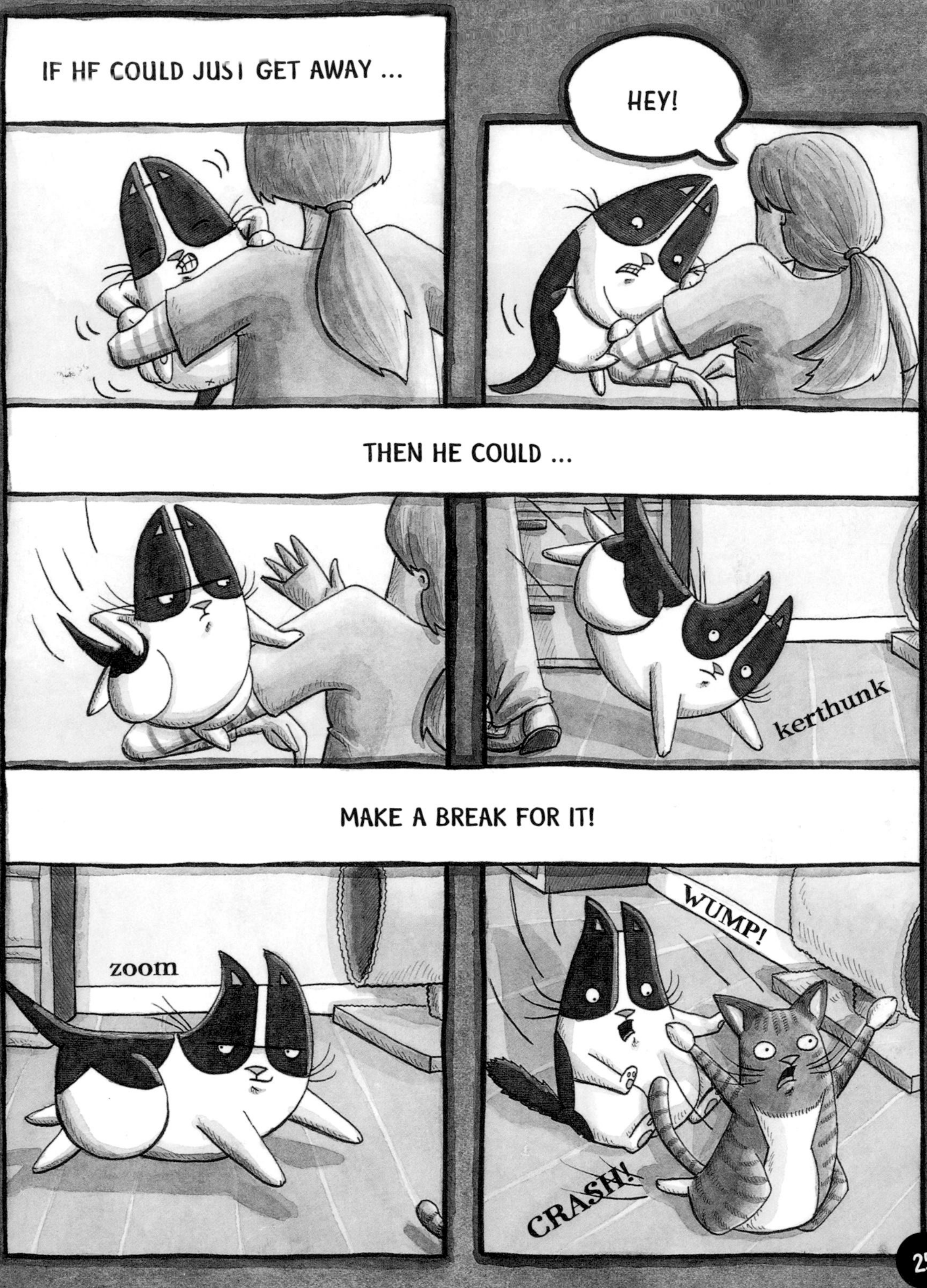
IF HE COULD JUST GET AWAY ...
HEY!
THEN HE COULD ...
kerthunk
MAKE A BREAK FOR IT!
zoom
WUMP!
CRASH!

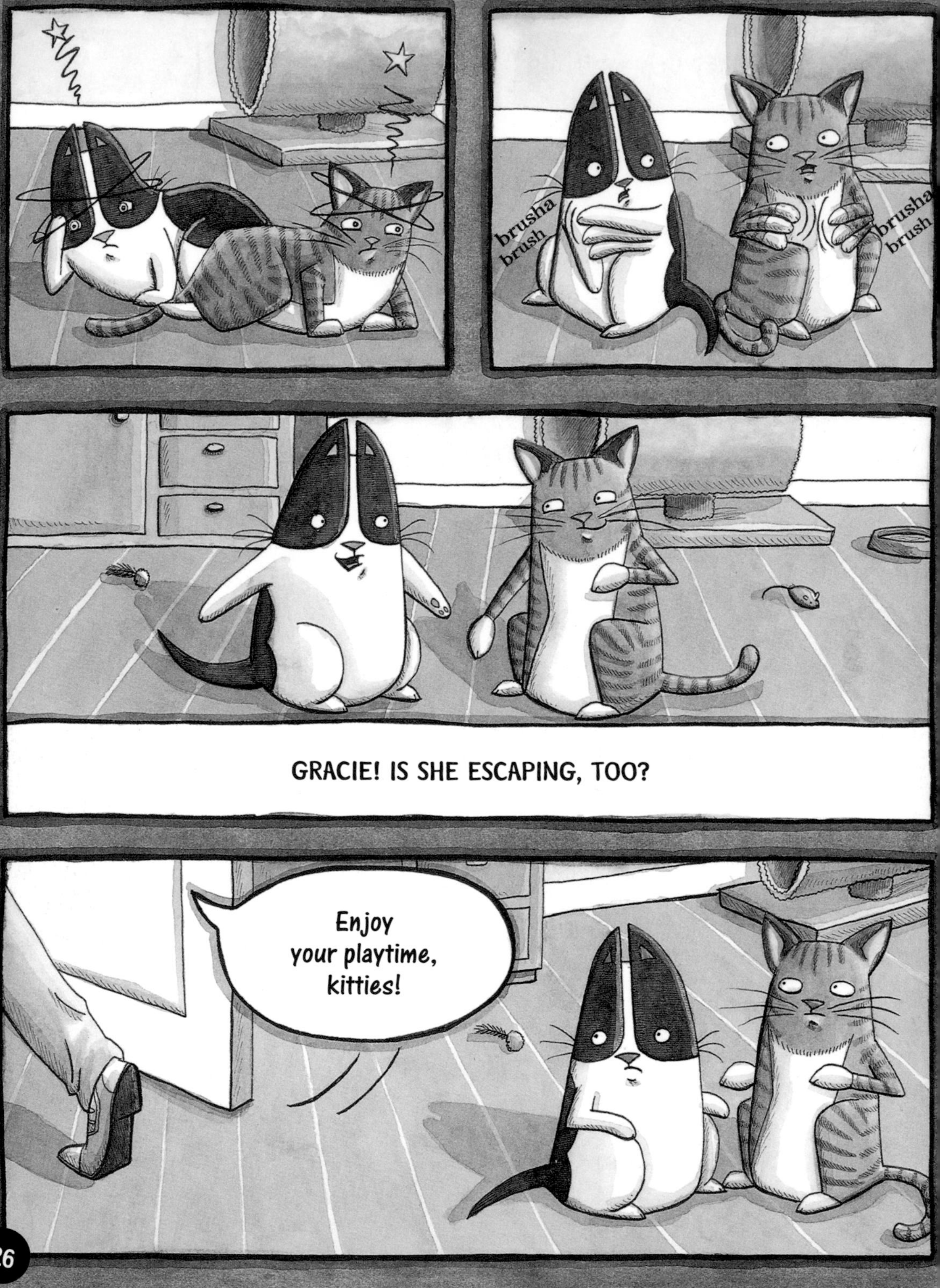
brusha
brush
brusha
brush
GRACIE! IS SHE ESCAPING, TOO?
Enjoy your playtime, kitties!

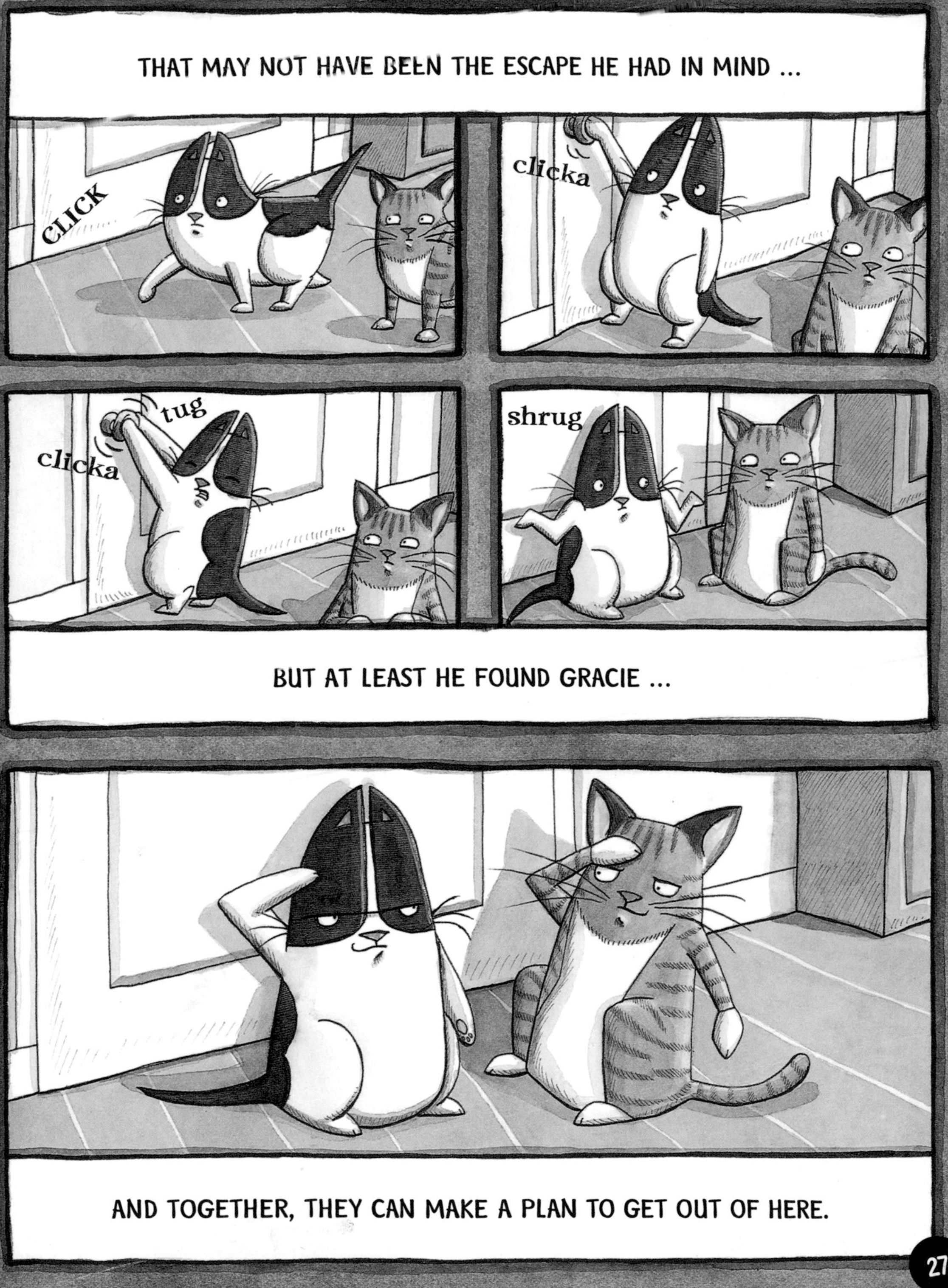
THAT MAY NOT HAVE BEEN THE ESCAPE HE HAD IN MIND ...
CLICK
clicka
clicka
tug
shrug
BUT AT LEAST HE FOUND GRACIE ...
AND TOGETHER, THEY CAN MAKE A PLAN TO GET OUT OF HERE.

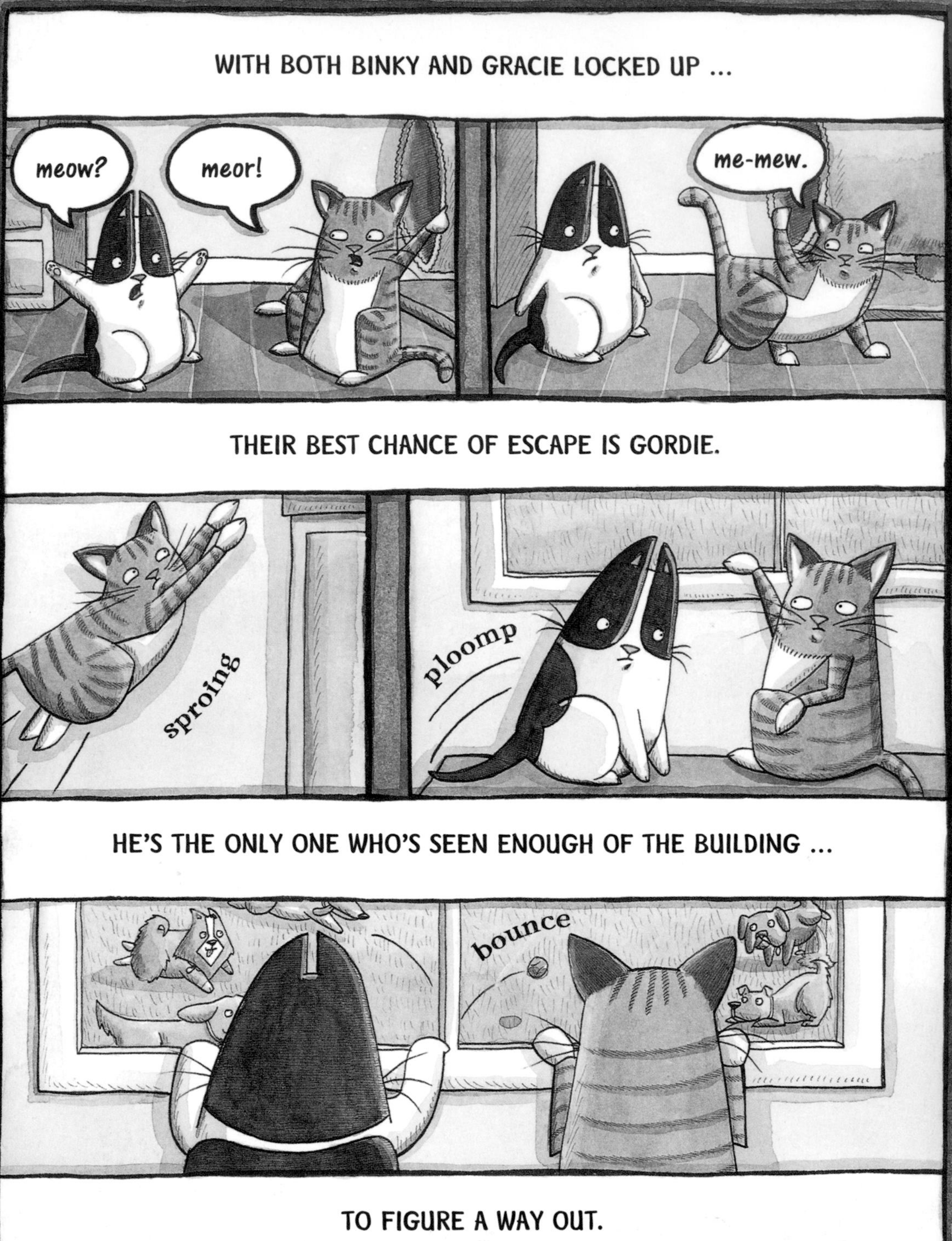
WITH BOTH BINKY AND GRACIE LOCKED UP ...
meow?
meor!
me-mew.
THEIR BEST CHANCE OF ESCAPE IS GORDIE.
sproing
ploomp
HE'S THE ONLY ONE WHO'S SEEN ENOUGH OF THE BUILDING ...
bounce
TO FIGURE A WAY OUT.

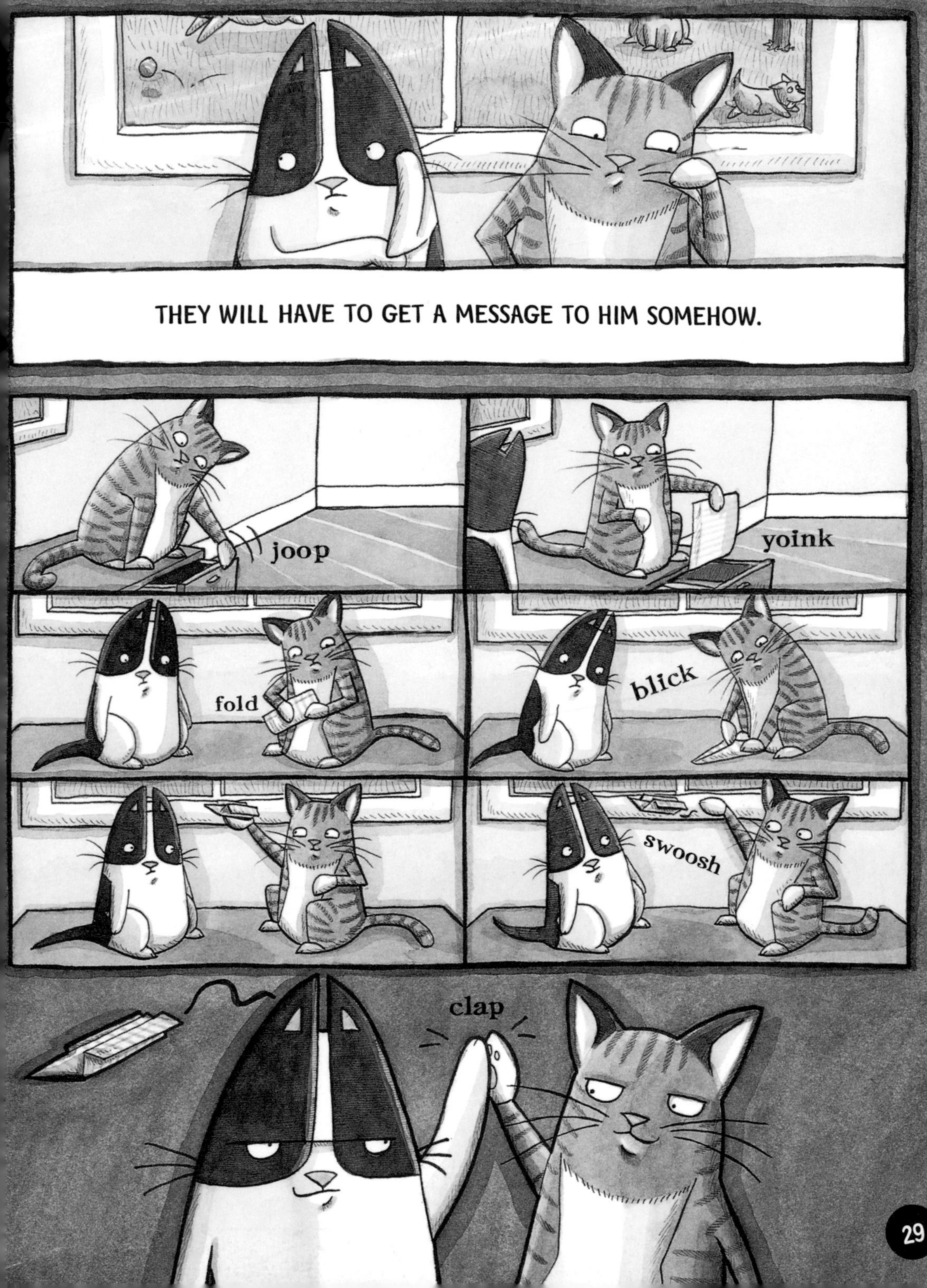
THEY WILL HAVE TO GET A MESSAGE TO HIM SOMEHOW.
joop
yoink
fold
blick
swoosh
clap

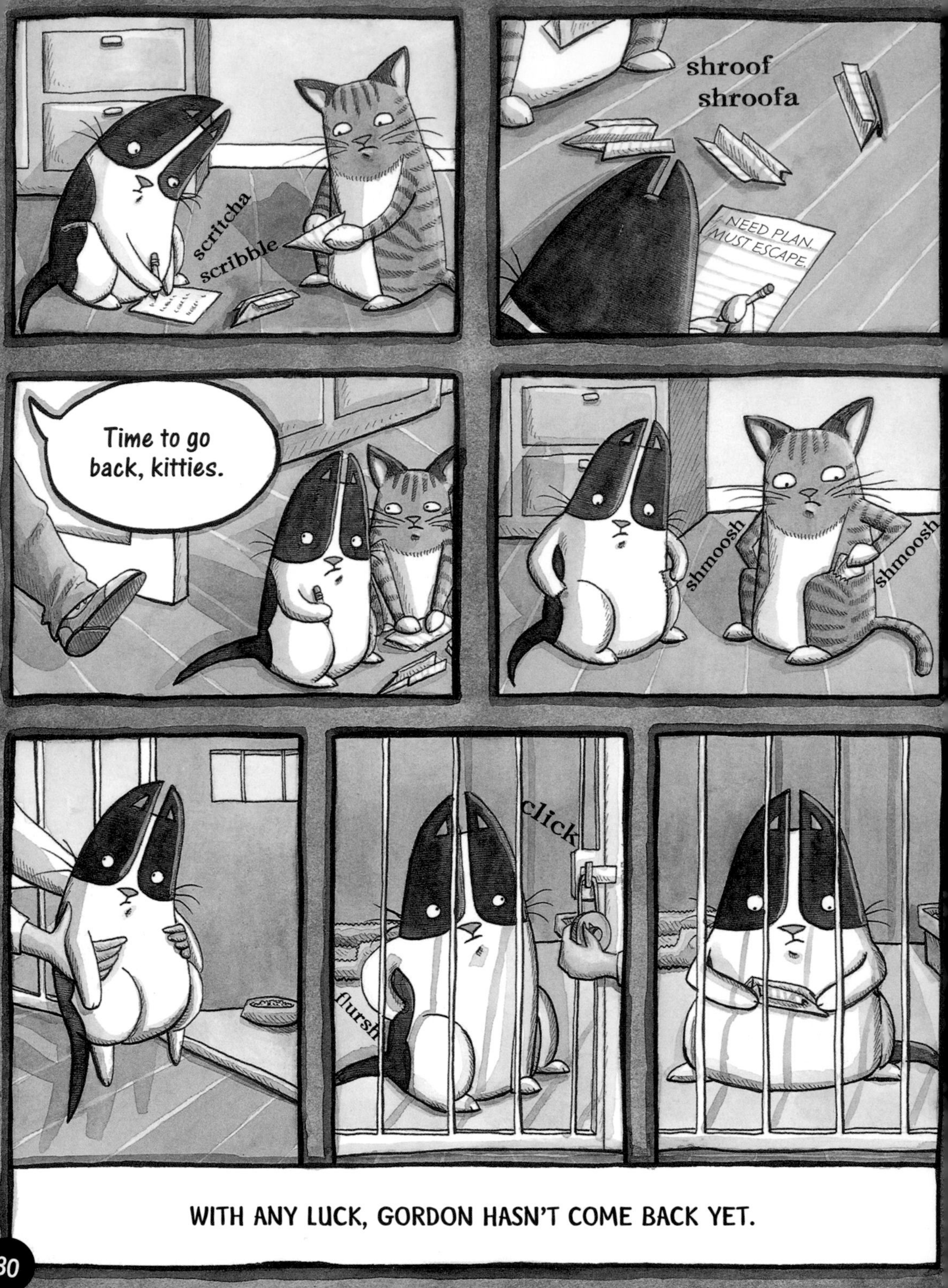
scritcha
scribble
shroof
shroofa
NEED PLAN.
MUST ESCAPE.
Time to go back, kitties.
shmoosh
shmoosh
click
flursh
WITH ANY LUCK, GORDON HASN'T COME BACK YET.

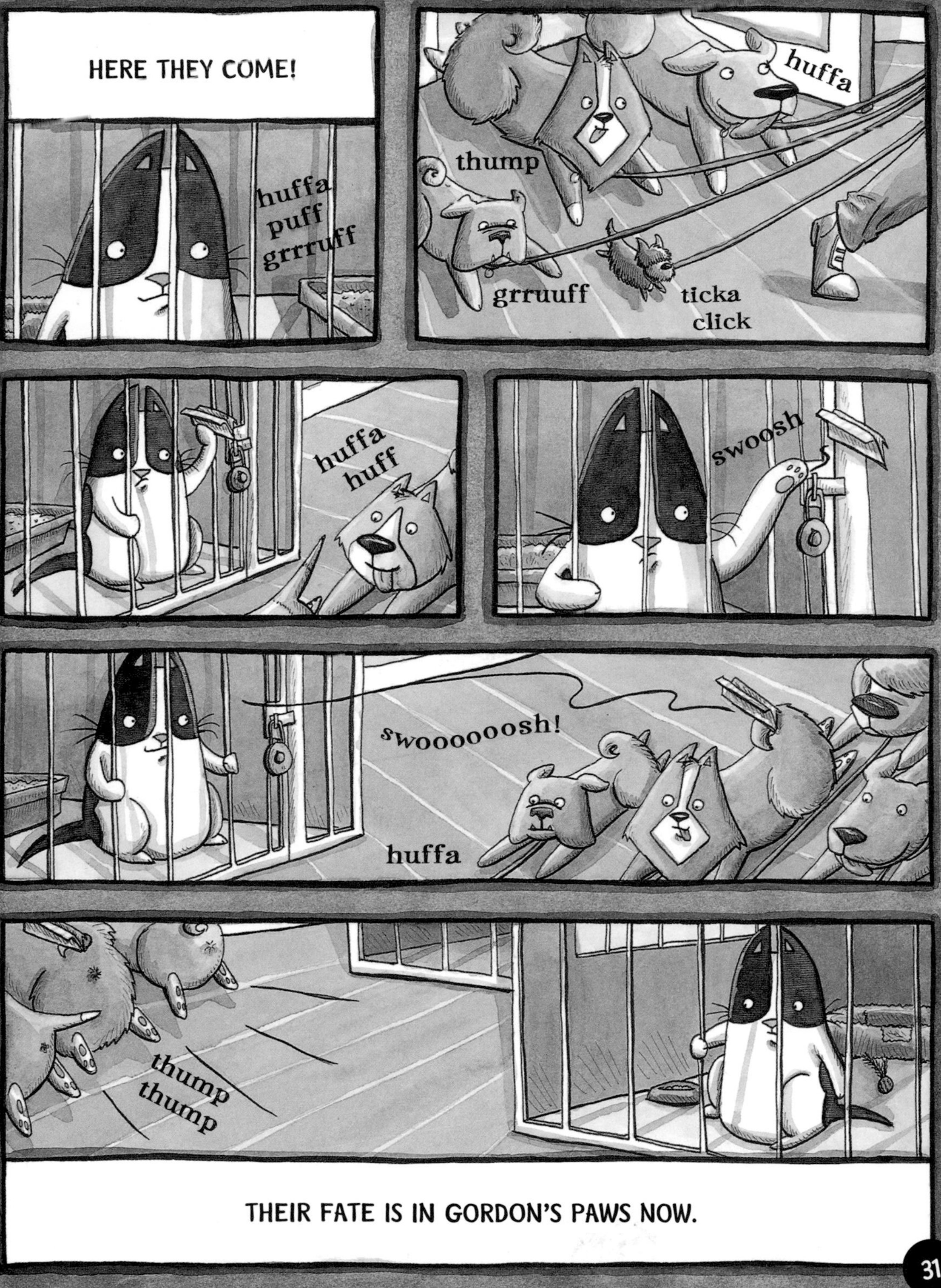
HERE THEY COME!
huffa
puff
grrruff
huffa
thump
grruuff
ticka
click
huffa
huff
swoosh
swoooooosh!
huffa
thump
thump
THEIR FATE IS IN GORDON'S PAWS NOW.

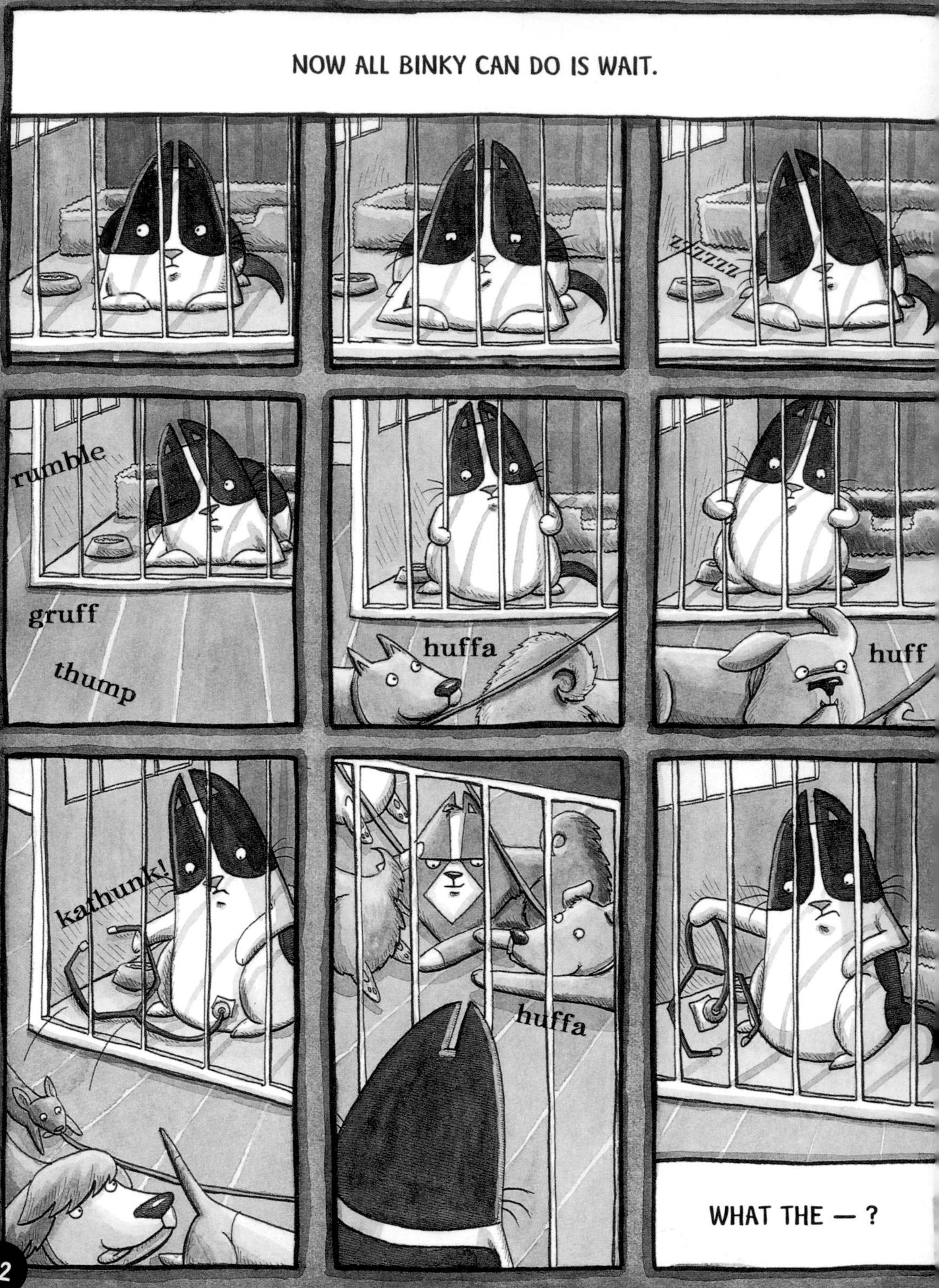
NOW ALL BINKY CAN DO IS WAIT.
zzzzzz
rumble
gruff
thump
huffa
huff
kathunk!
huffa
WHAT THE — ?

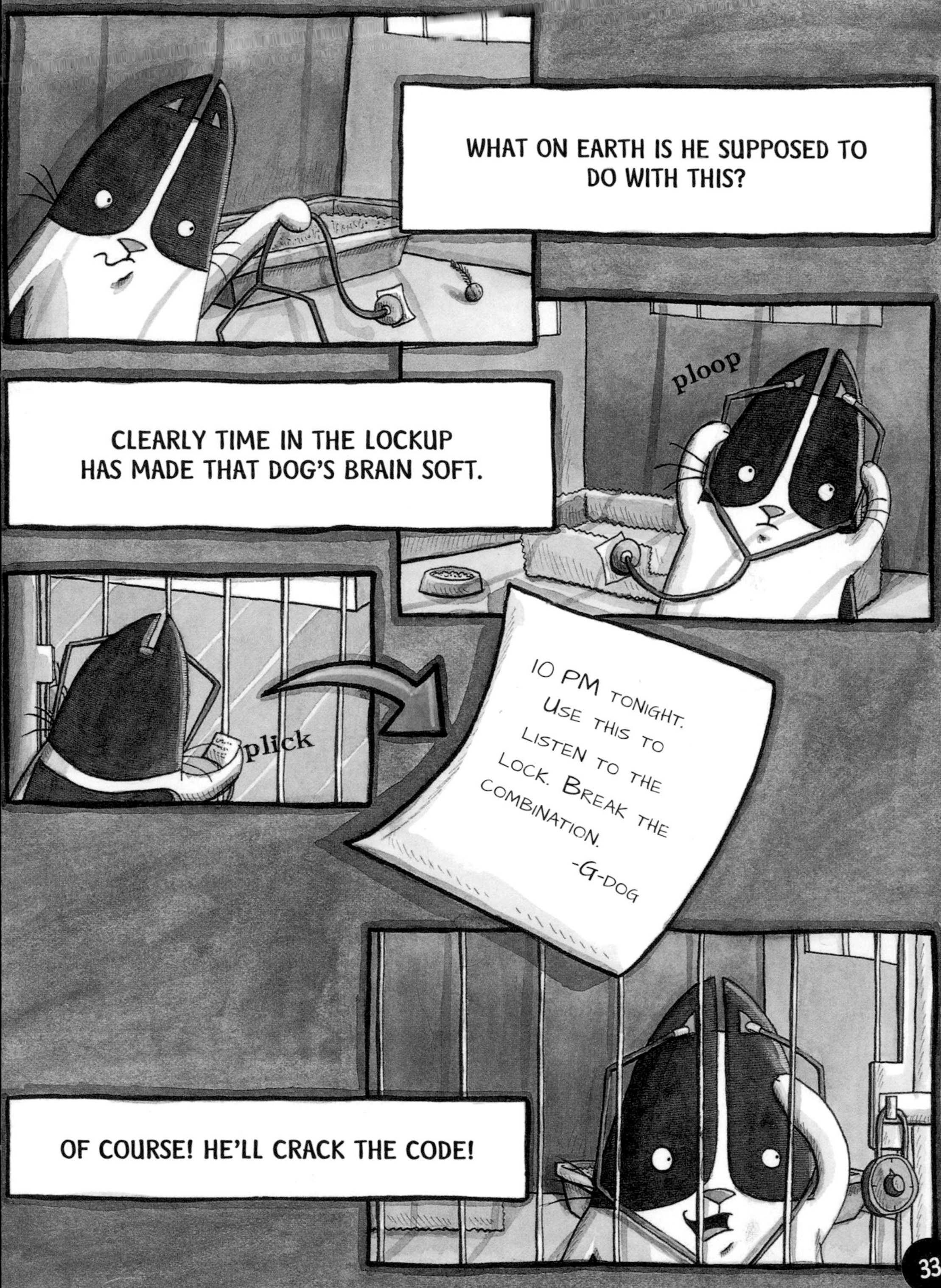
WHAT ON EARTH IS HE SUPPOSED TO DO WITH THIS?
CLEARLY TIME IN THE LOCKUP HAS MADE THAT DOG'S BRAIN SOFT.
ploop
plick
10 PM TONIGHT. USE THIS TO LISTEN TO THE LOCK. BREAK THE COMBINATION.
-G-DOG
OF COURSE! HE'LL CRACK THE CODE!

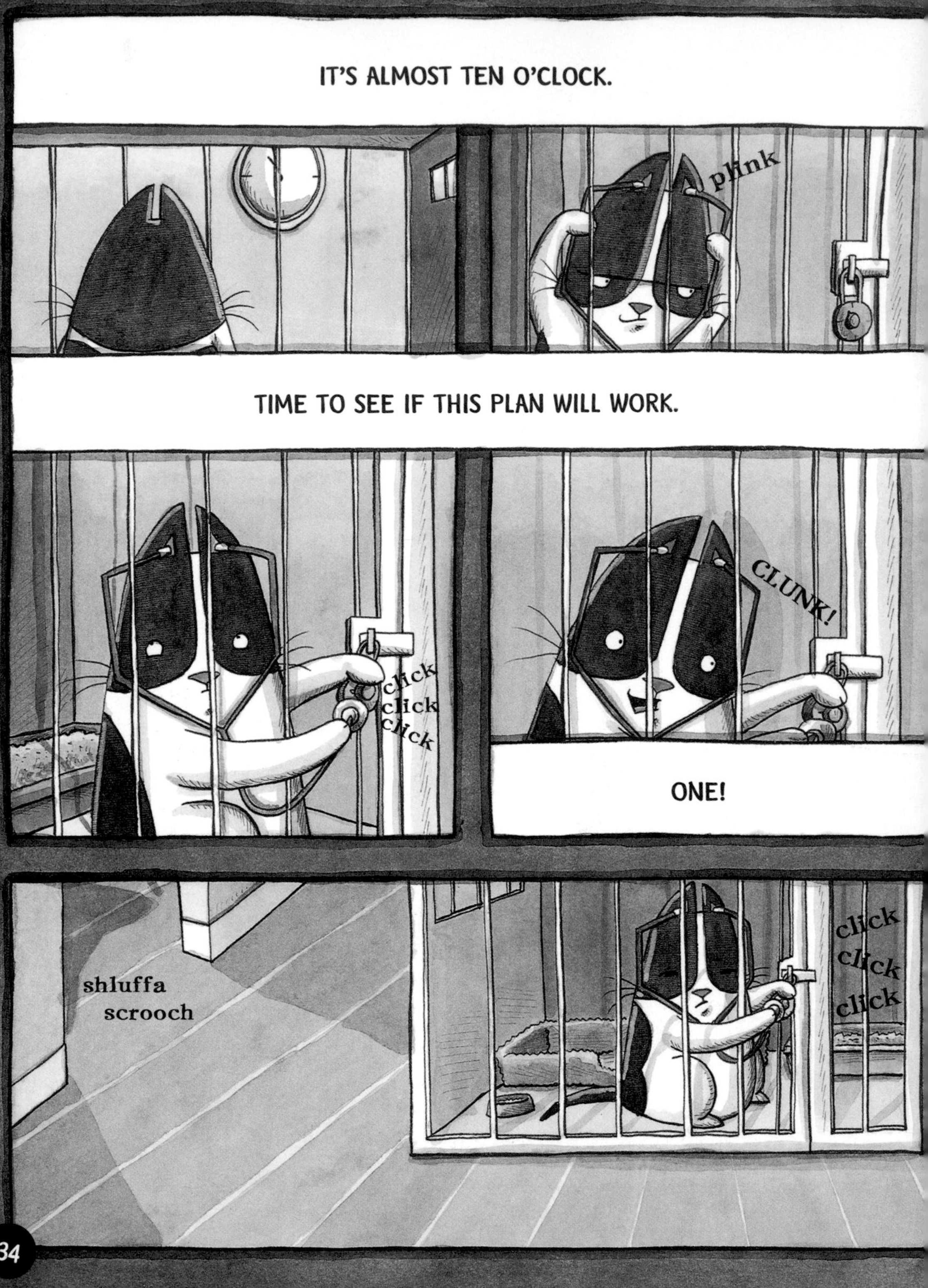
IT'S ALMOST TEN O'CLOCK.
plink
TIME TO SEE IF THIS PLAN WILL WORK.
click
click
click
CLUNK!
ONE!
shluffa
scrooch
click
click
click

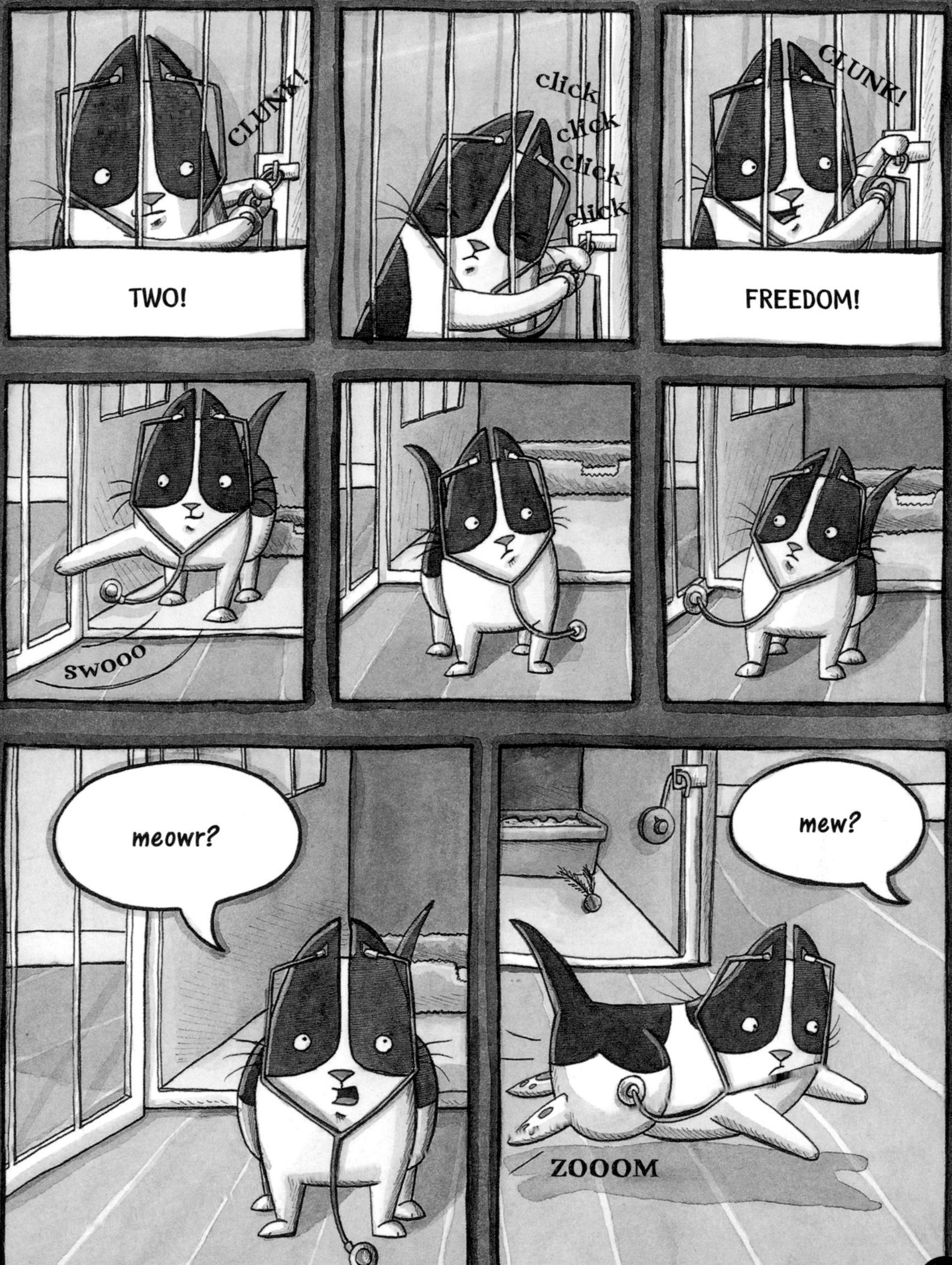
CLUNK!
TWO!
click
click
click
click
CLUNK!
FREEDOM!
SWOOO
meowr?
mew?
ZOOOM

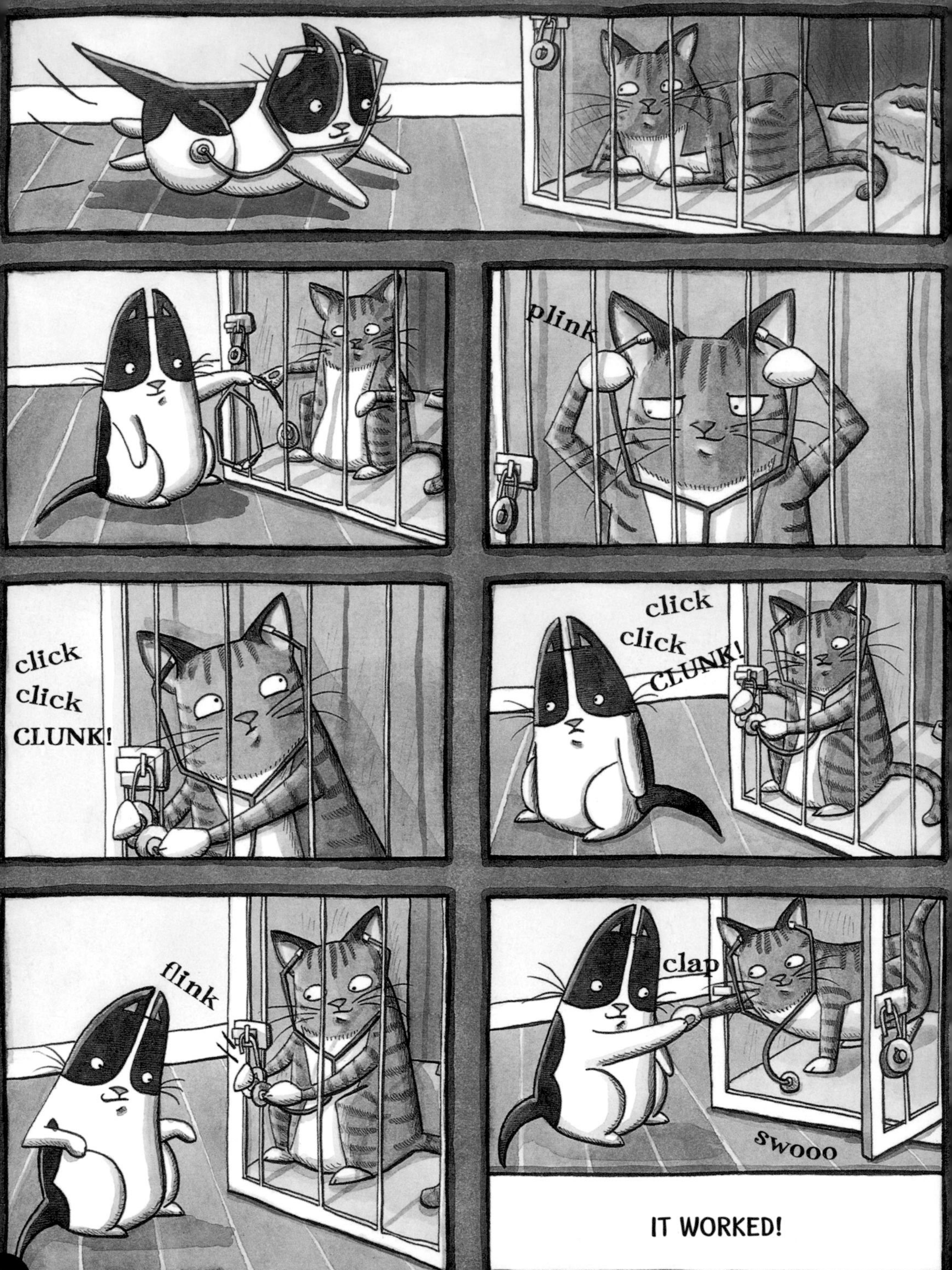
plink
click
click
CLUNK!
click
click
CLUNK!
flink
clap
swooo
IT WORKED!

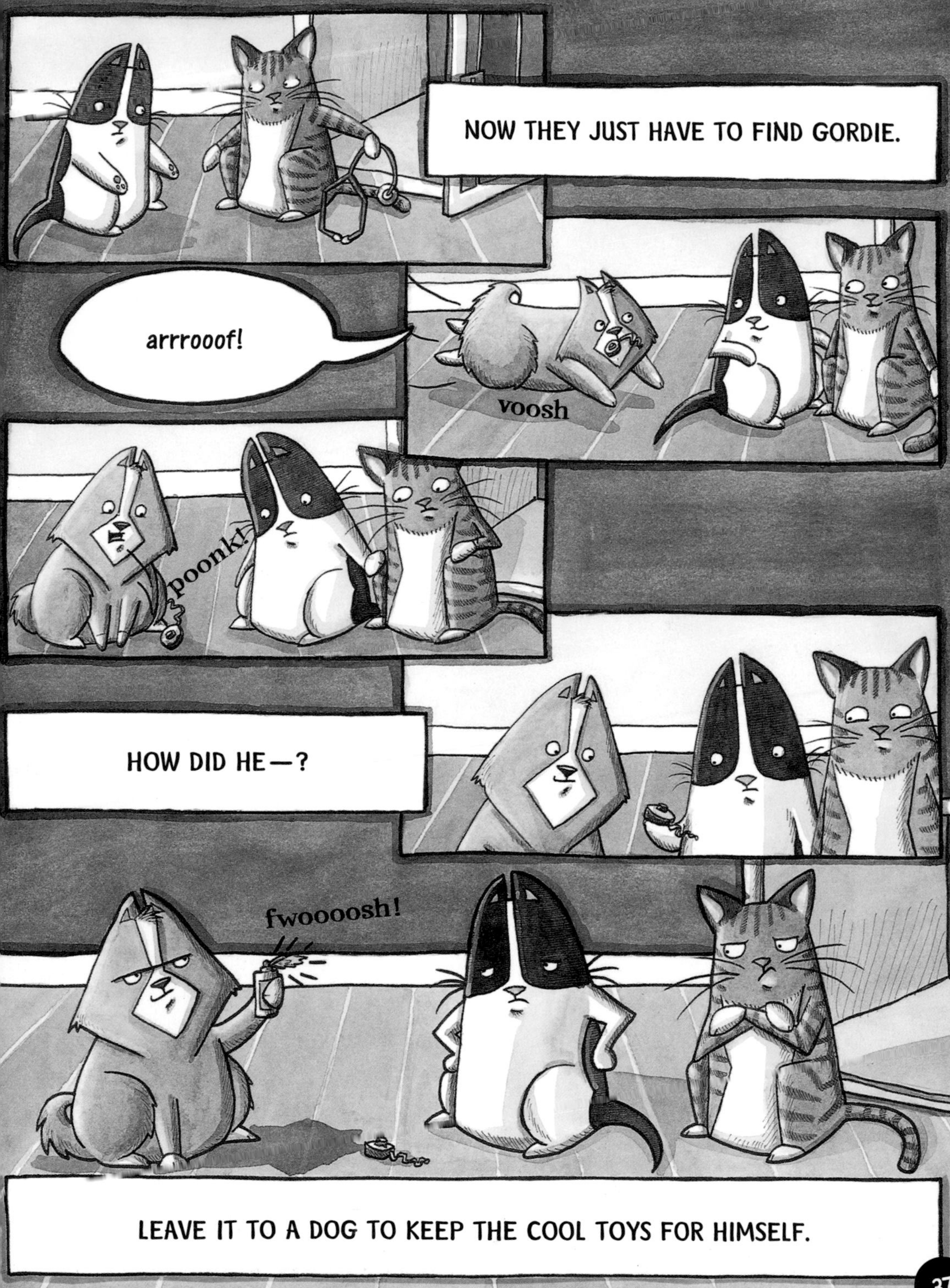
NOW THEY JUST HAVE TO FIND GORDIE.
arrrooof!
voosh
poonk!
HOW DID HE—?
fwooooosh!
LEAVE IT TO A DOG TO KEEP THE COOL TOYS FOR HIMSELF.

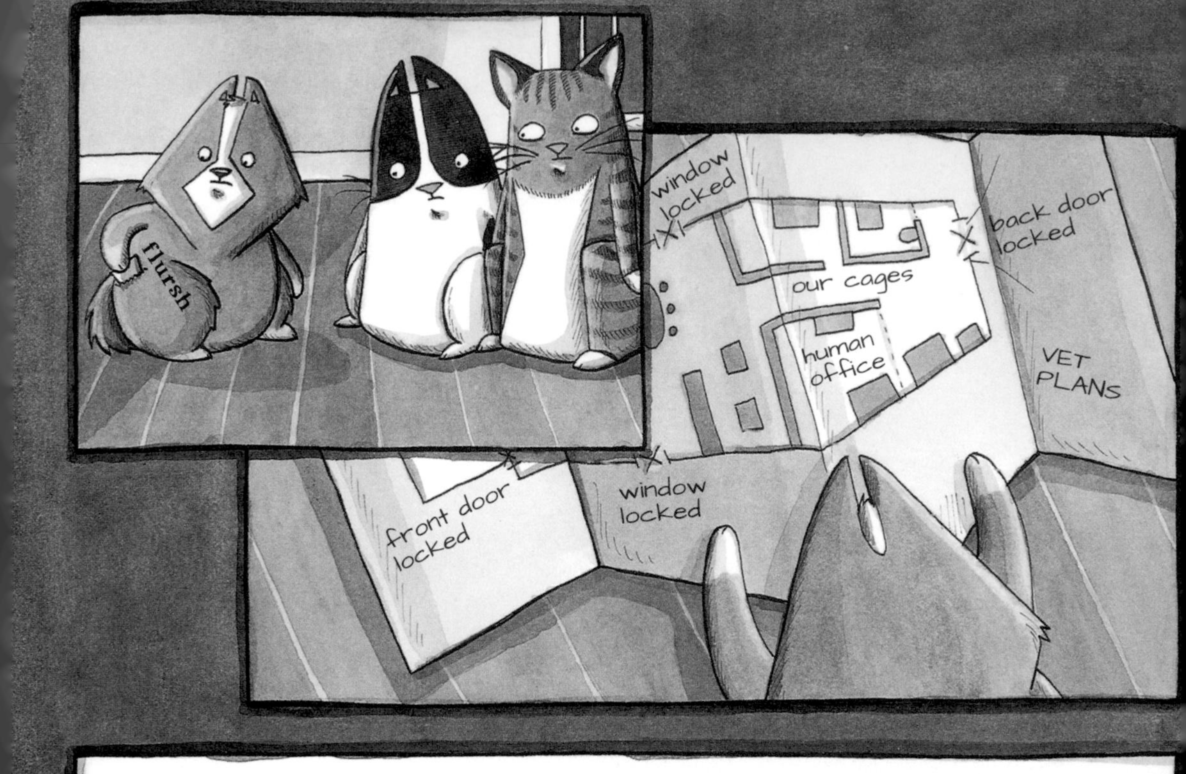
flursh
window locked
back door locked
our cages
human office
VET PLANS
front door locked
window locked

THE VENTS ARE THEIR BEST CHANCE FOR ESCAPE.

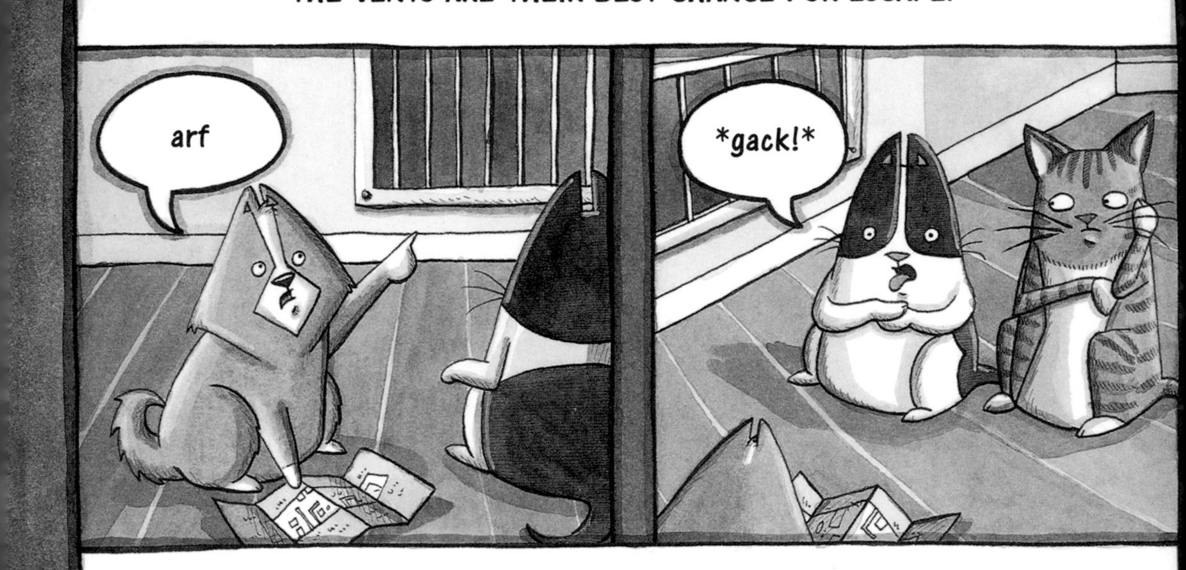
arf
gack!

BUT HOW WILL THEY BREATHE IN **OUTER SPACE?**

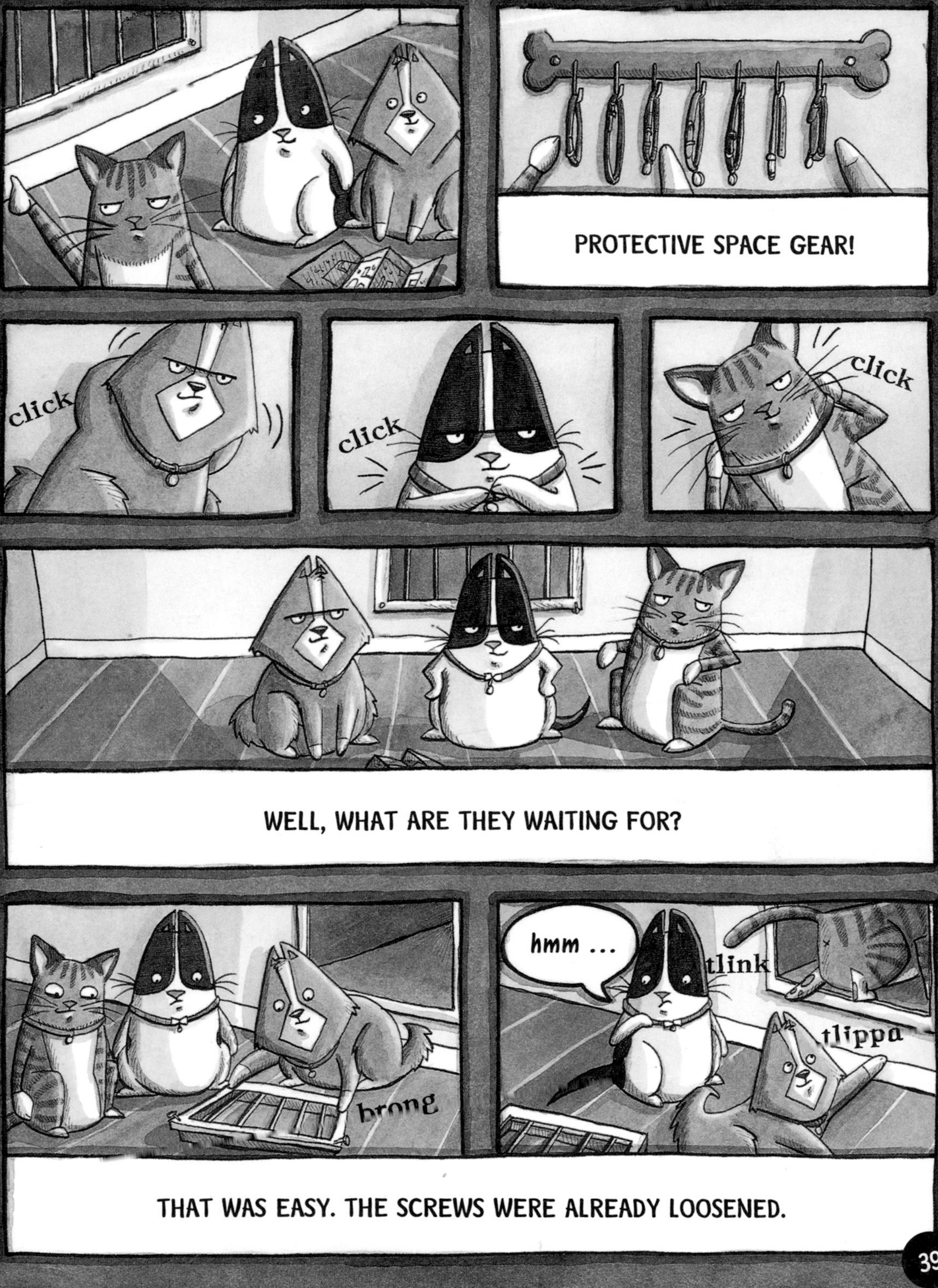
PROTECTIVE SPACE GEAR!
click
click
click
WELL, WHAT ARE THEY WAITING FOR?
brong
hmm ...
tlink
tlippa
THAT WAS EASY. THE SCREWS WERE ALREADY LOOSENED.

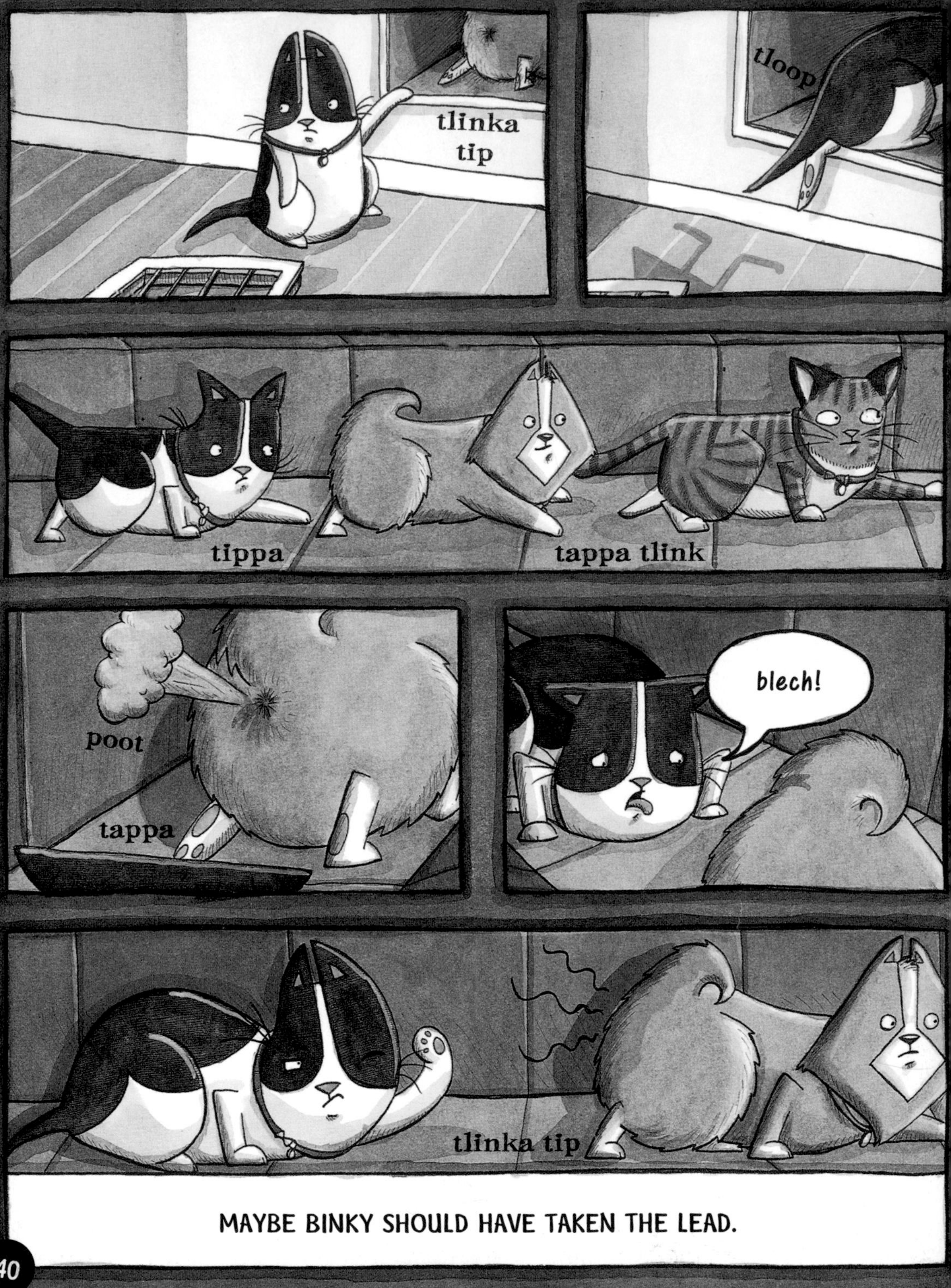
tlinka
tip
tloop
tippa
tappa tlink
poot
tappa
blech!
tlinka tip
MAYBE BINKY SHOULD HAVE TAKEN THE LEAD.

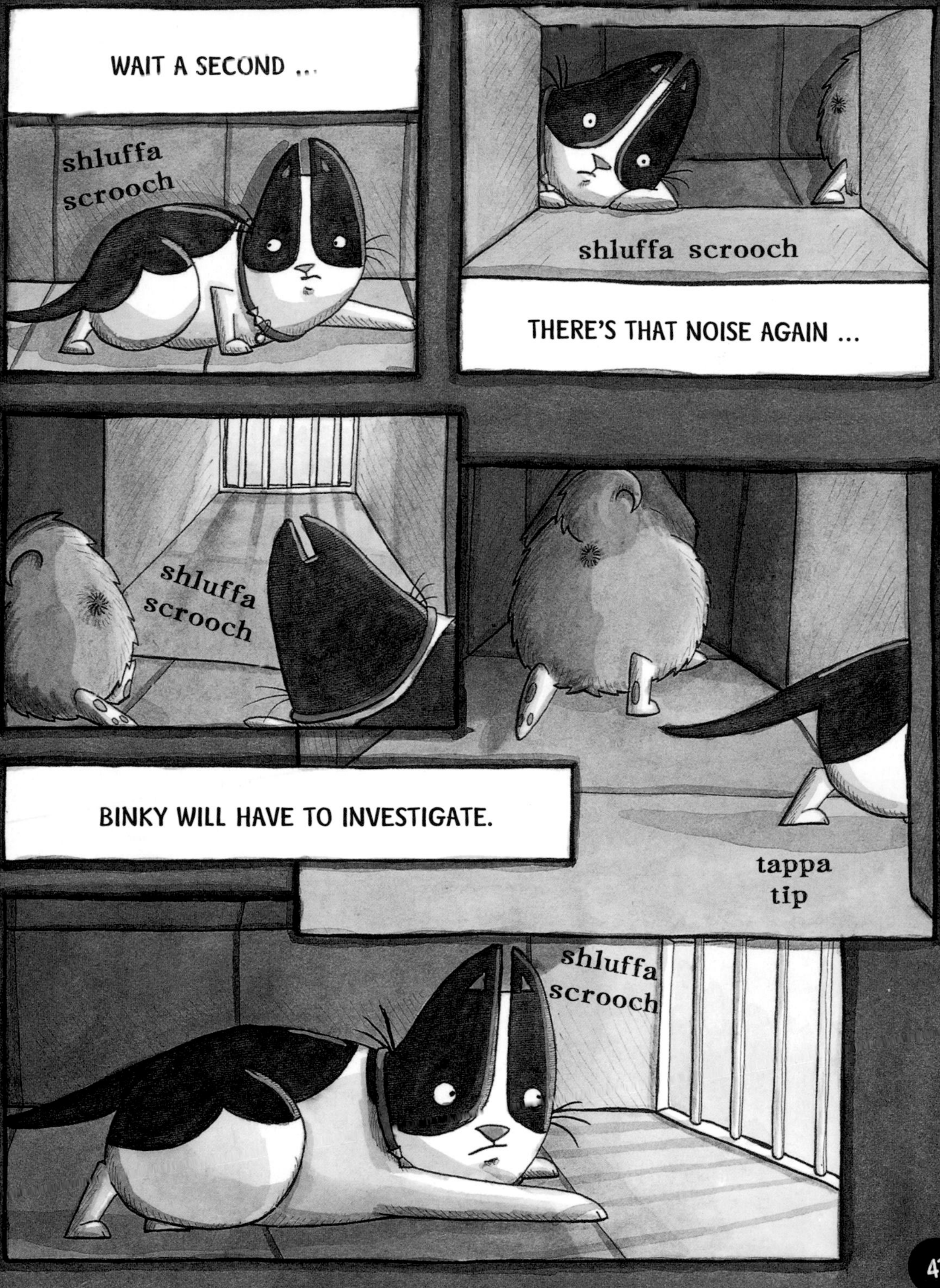
WAIT A SECOND ...
shluffa scrooch
shluffa scrooch
THERE'S THAT NOISE AGAIN ...
shluffa scrooch
BINKY WILL HAVE TO INVESTIGATE.
tappa tip
shluffa scrooch

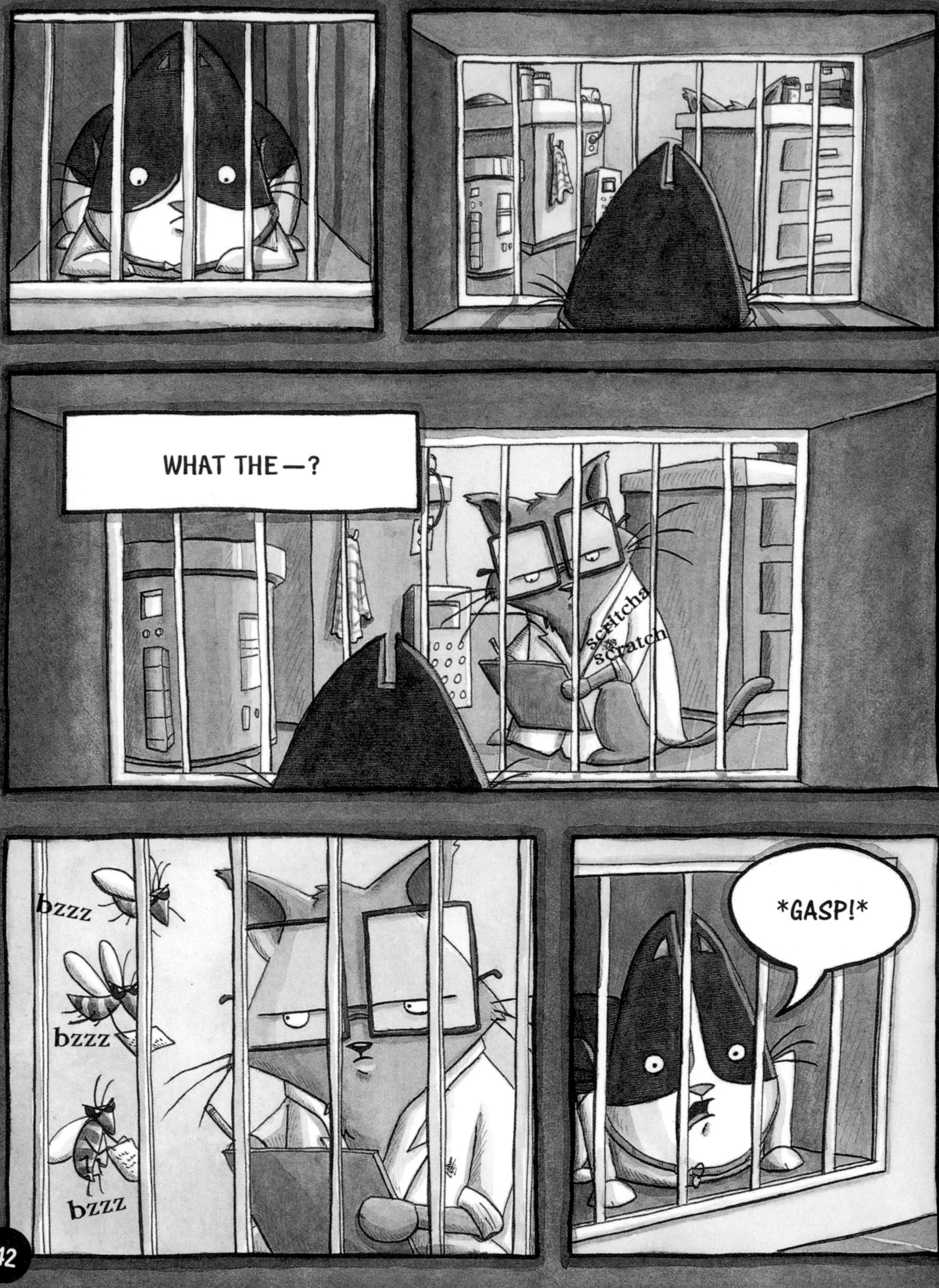
WHAT THE—?
scritcha
scratch
bzzz
bzzz
bzzz
GASP!

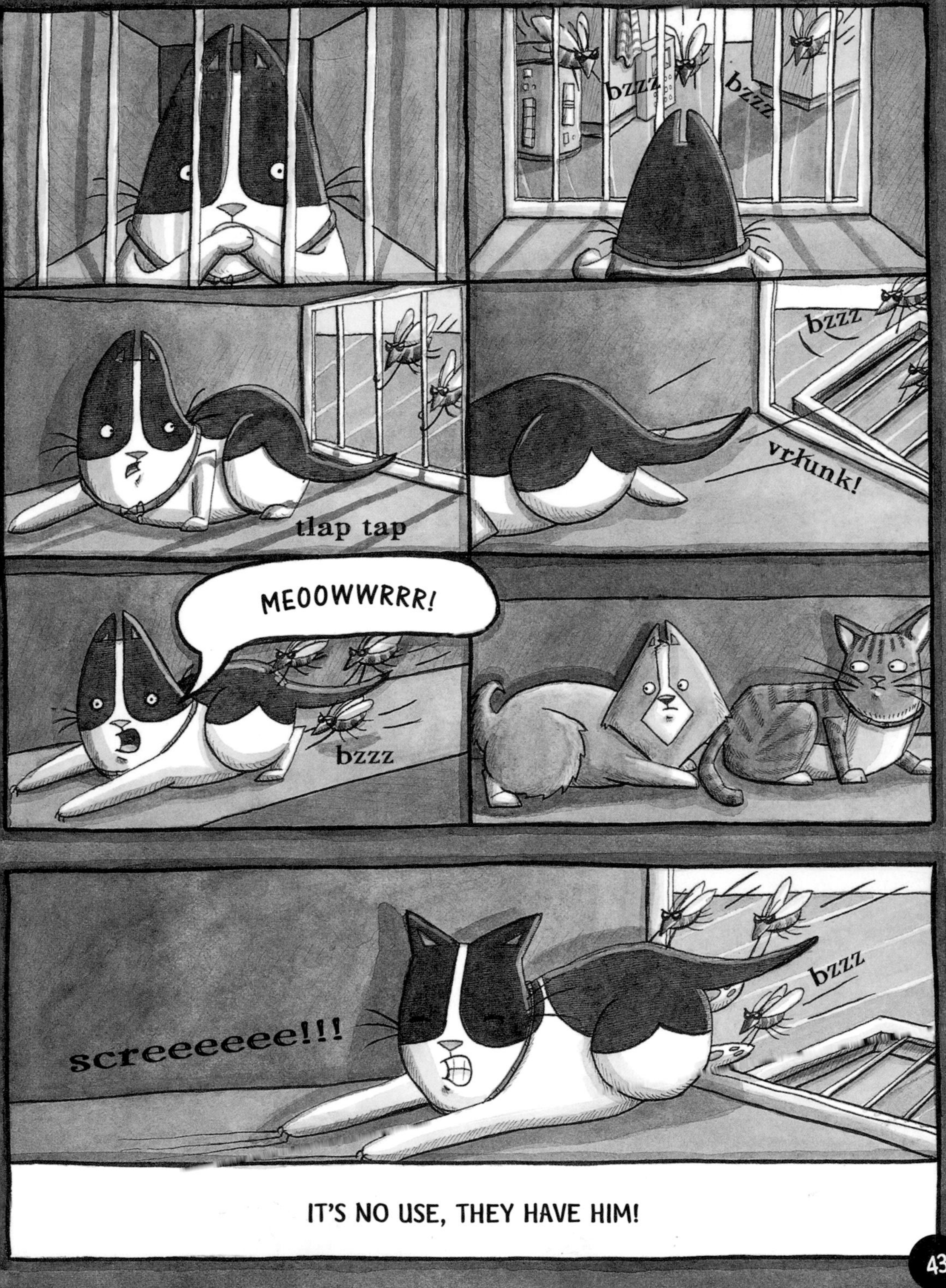
bzzz
bzzz
tlap tap
bzzz
vrlunk!
MEOOWWRRR!
bzzz
screeeeeee!!!
bzzz
IT'S NO USE, THEY HAVE HIM!

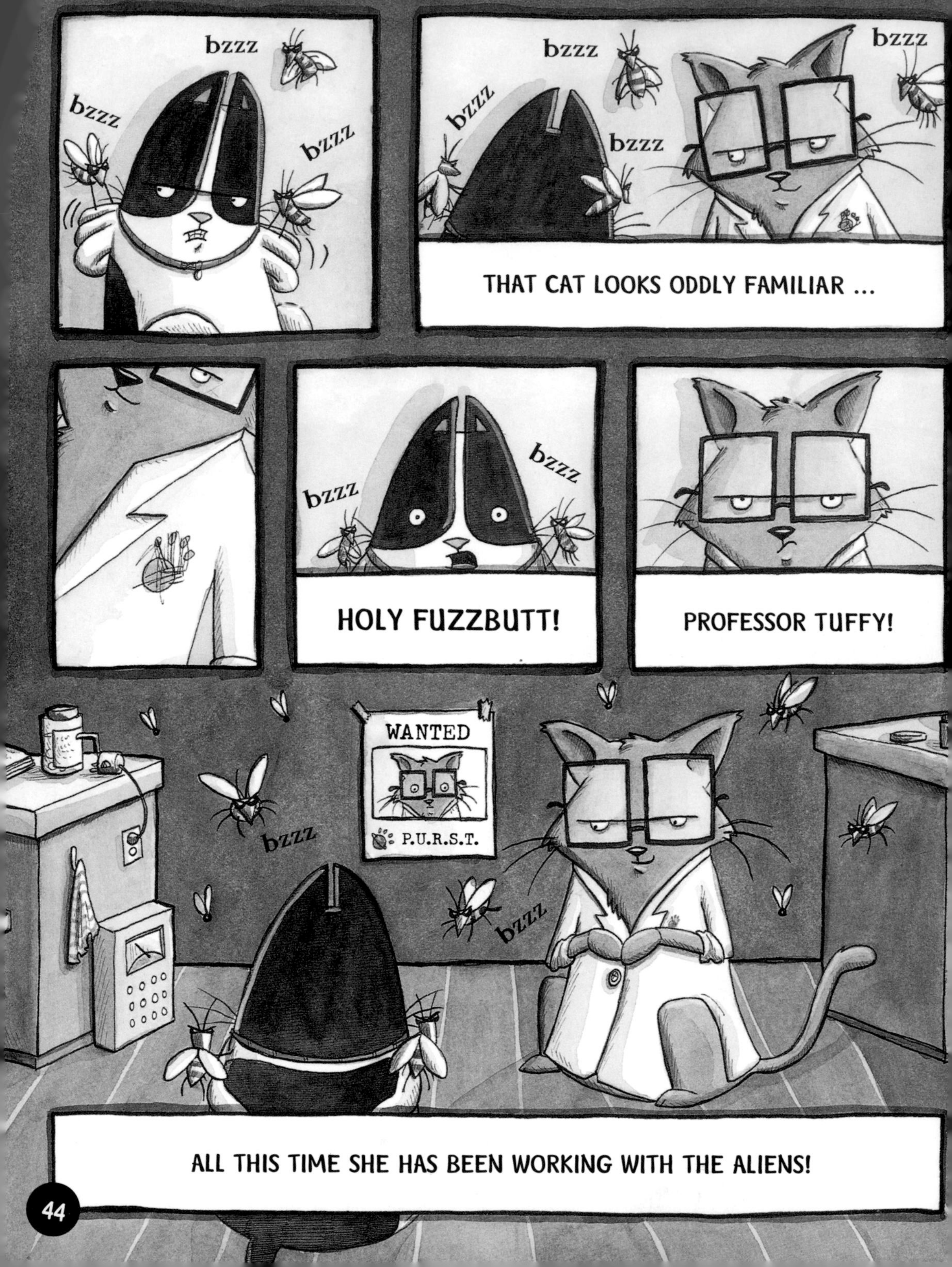
bzzz
bzzz
bzzz
bzzz
bzzz
bzzz
bzzz
THAT CAT LOOKS ODDLY FAMILIAR ...
bzzz
bzzz
HOLY FUZZBUTT!
PROFESSOR TUFFY!
WANTED
P.U.R.S.T.
bzzz
bzzz
ALL THIS TIME SHE HAS BEEN WORKING WITH THE ALIENS!

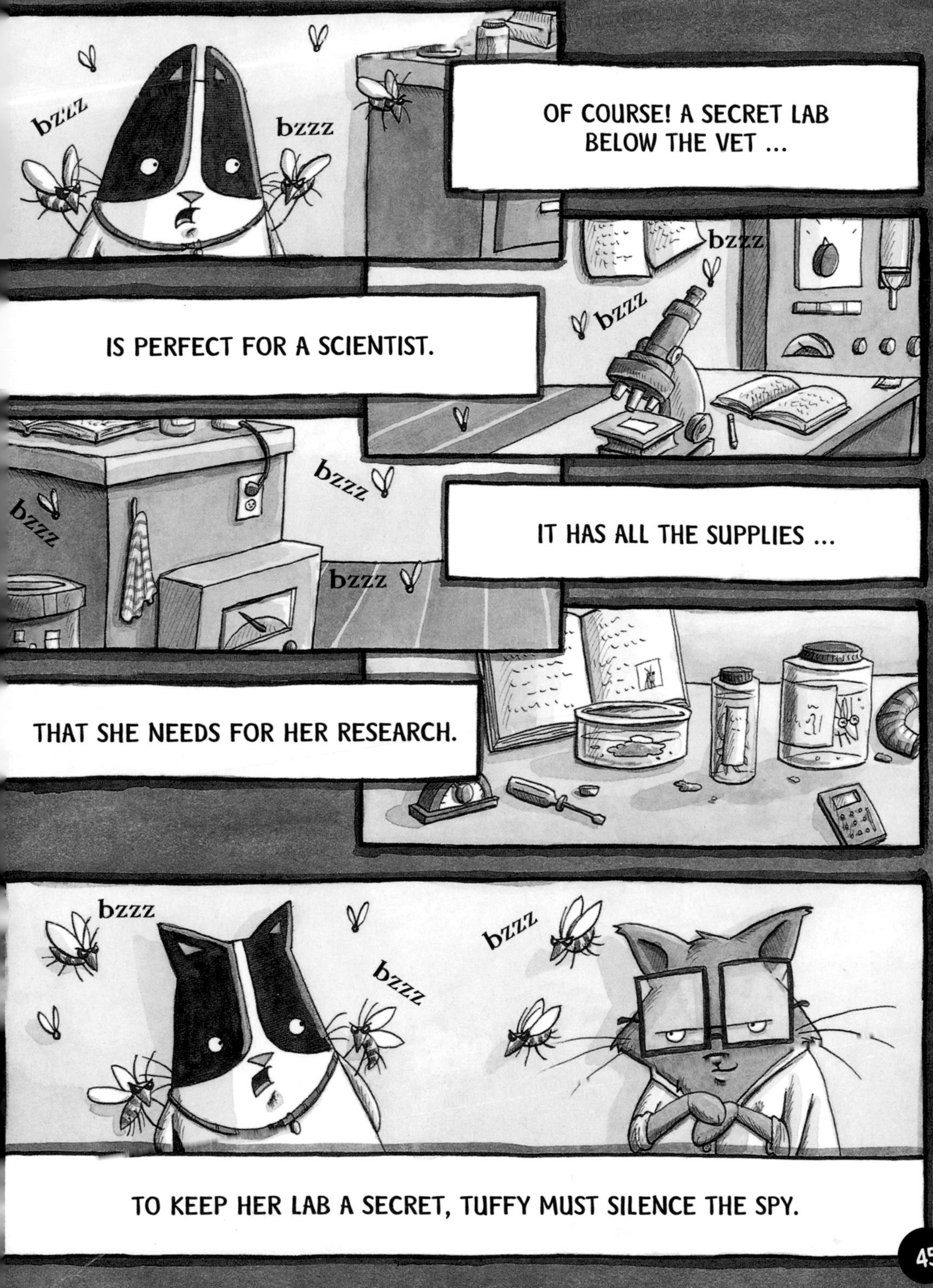

bzzz
bzzz
OF COURSE! A SECRET LAB BELOW THE VET ...
bzzz
bzzz
IS PERFECT FOR A SCIENTIST.
bzzz
bzzz
bzzz
IT HAS ALL THE SUPPLIES ...
THAT SHE NEEDS FOR HER RESEARCH.
bzzz
bzzz
bzzz
TO KEEP HER LAB A SECRET, TUFFY MUST SILENCE THE SPY.

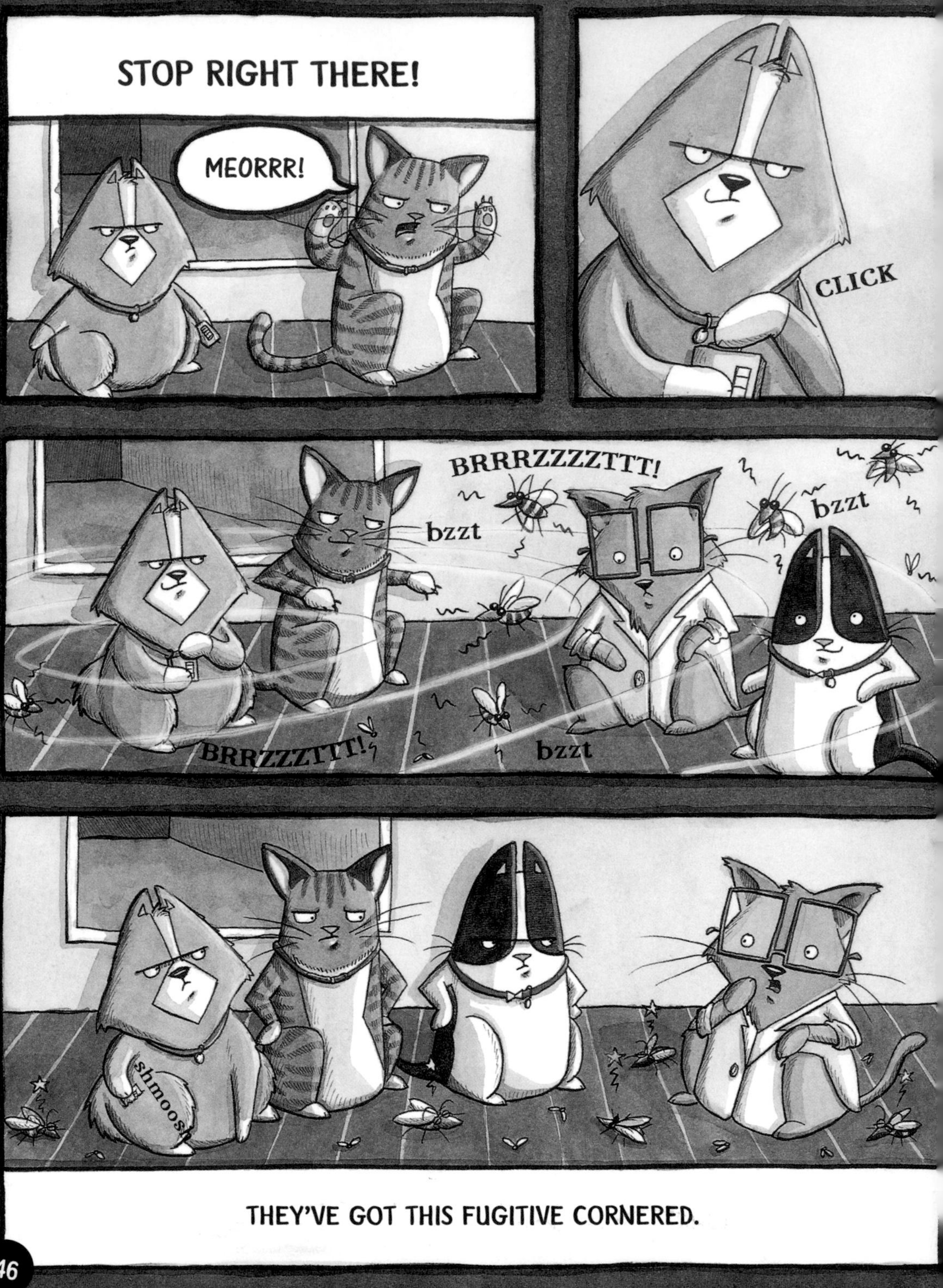
STOP RIGHT THERE!
MEORRR!
CLICK
BRRRZZZZTTT!
bzzt
bzzt
BRRZZZTTT!
bzzt
shmoos
THEY'VE GOT THIS FUGITIVE CORNERED.

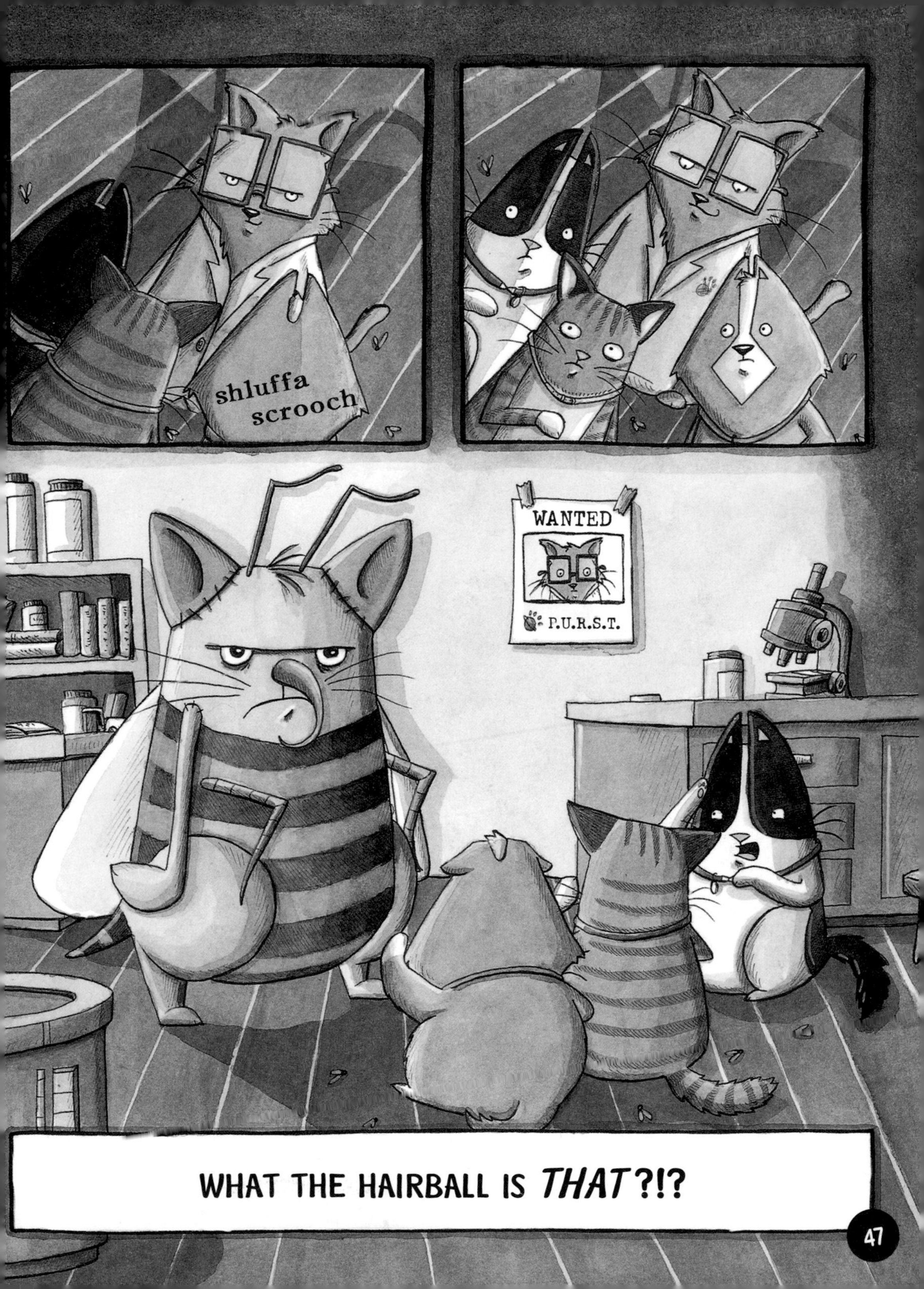
shluffa
scrooch
WANTED
P.U.R.S.T.
WHAT THE HAIRBALL IS *THAT*?!?

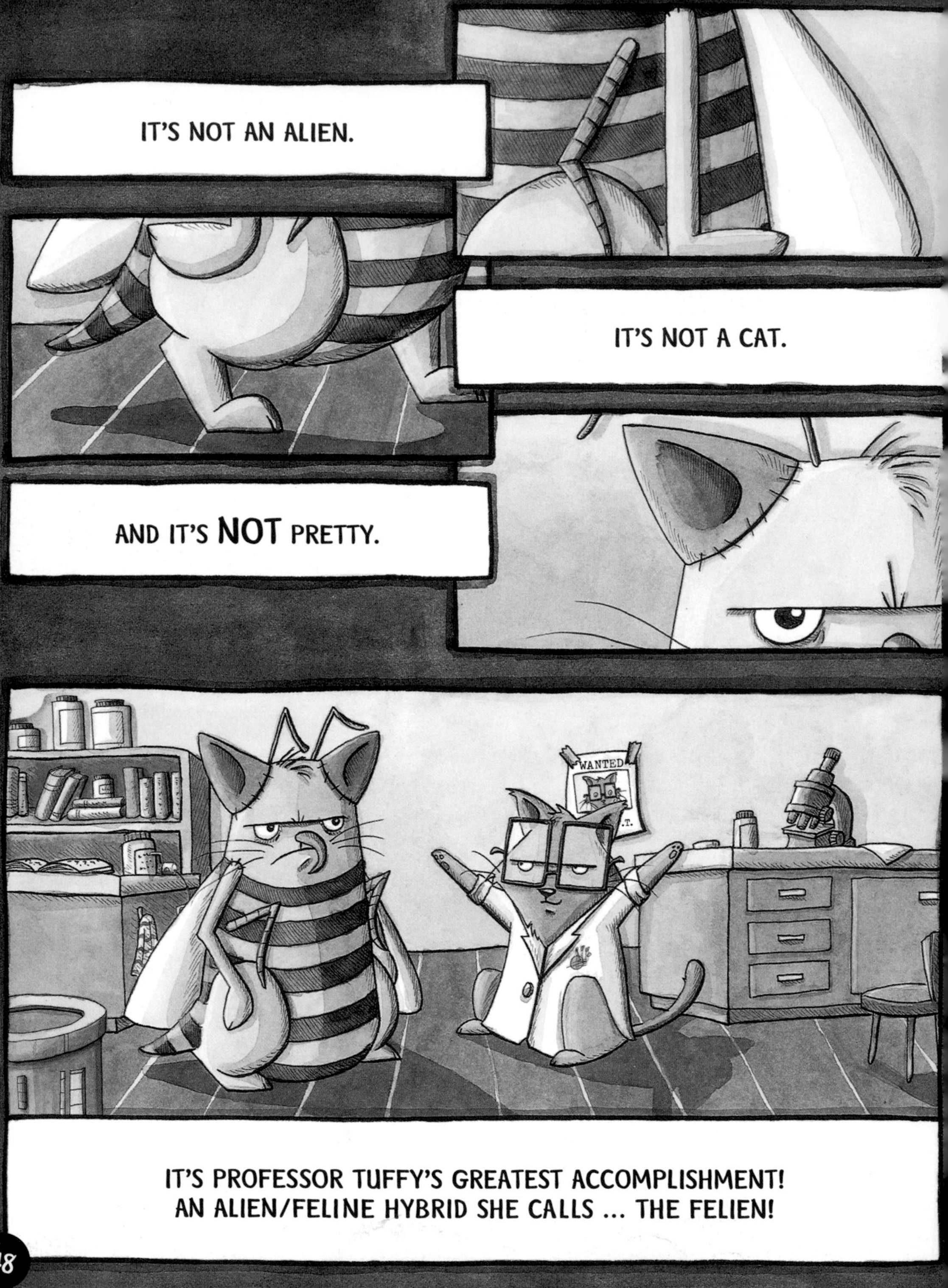
IT'S NOT AN ALIEN.
IT'S NOT A CAT.
AND IT'S NOT PRETTY.
WANTED
IT'S PROFESSOR TUFFY'S GREATEST ACCOMPLISHMENT! AN ALIEN/FELINE HYBRID SHE CALLS ... THE FELIEN!

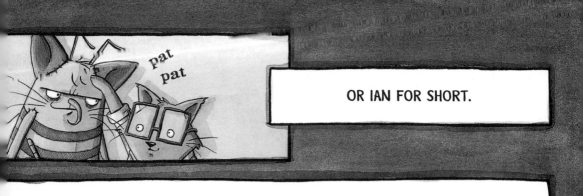

pat
pat
OR IAN FOR SHORT.
HE IS DESIGNED TO INFILTRATE AND HELP OVERTAKE ANY SPACE STATION!
Hi, kitty!
bzzzzzzzzzz
Yipes!
BUT WHAT ABOUT HER OATH TO — ?
TUFFY DOESN'T CARE ABOUT PROTECTING HUMANS!
HER HUMANS DIDN'T PROTECT *HER*.

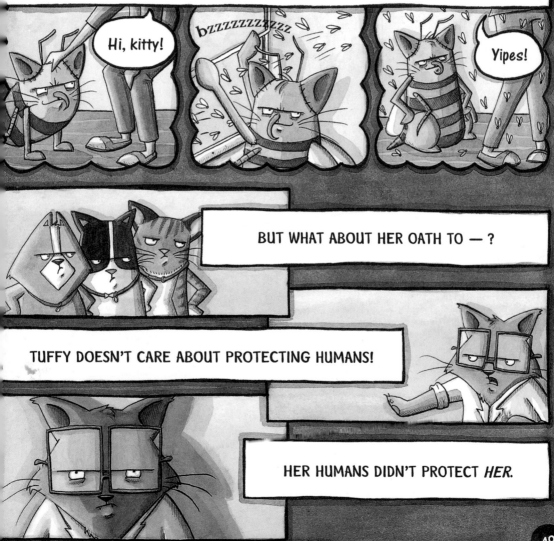

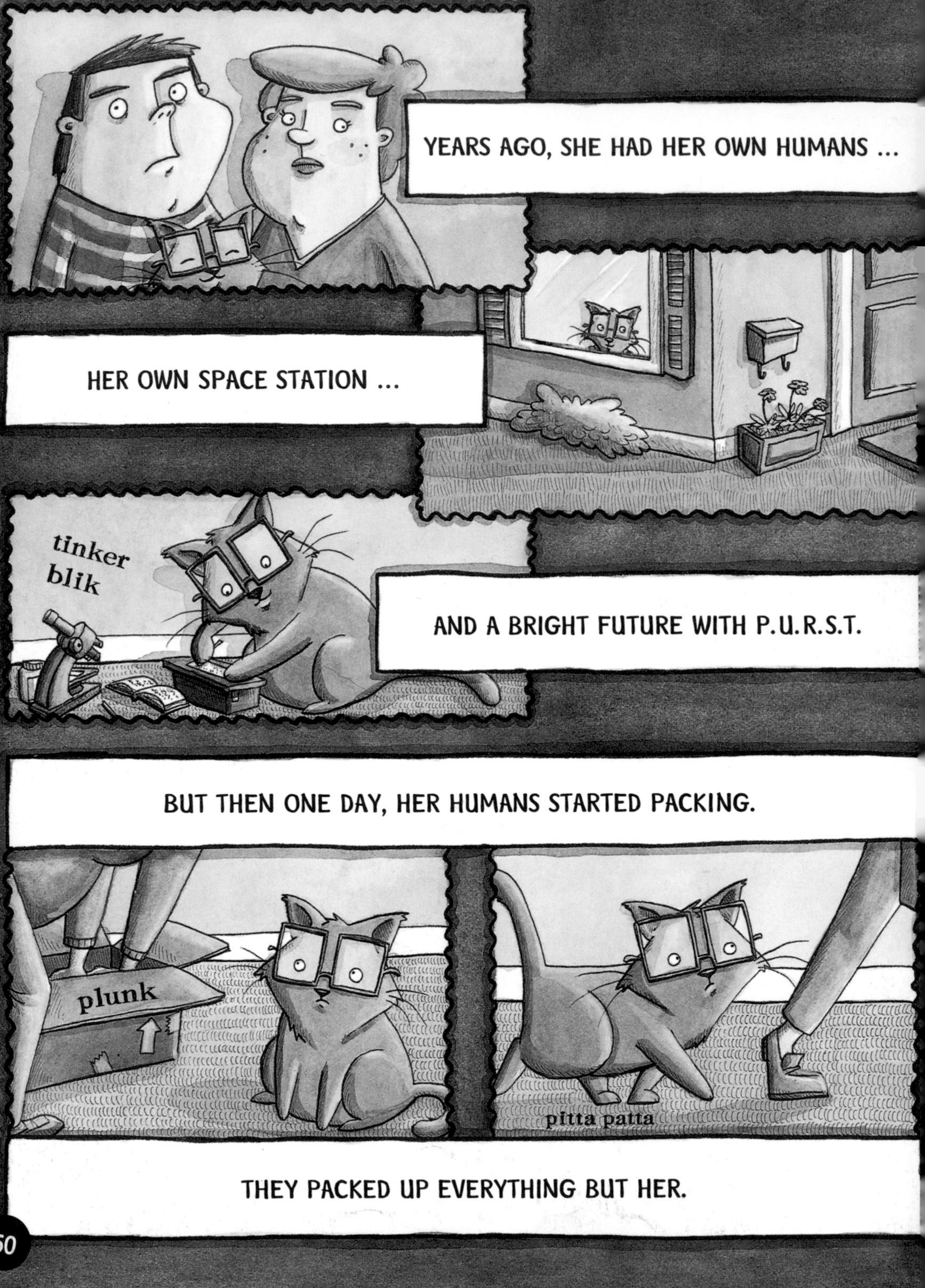
YEARS AGO, SHE HAD HER OWN HUMANS ...
HER OWN SPACE STATION ...
tinker
blik
AND A BRIGHT FUTURE WITH P.U.R.S.T.
BUT THEN ONE DAY, HER HUMANS STARTED PACKING.
plunk
pitta patta
THEY PACKED UP EVERYTHING BUT HER.

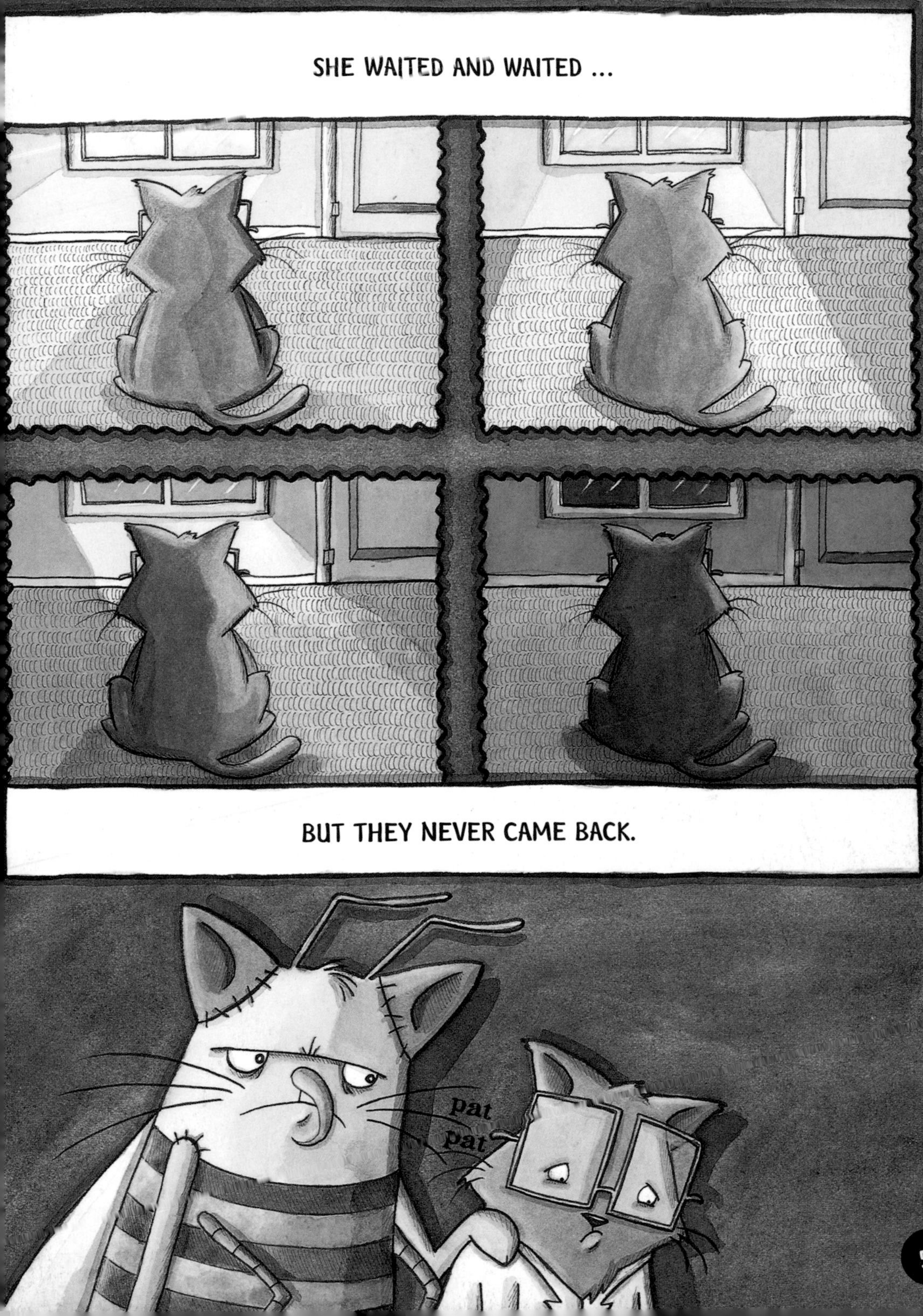
SHE WAITED AND WAITED ...
BUT THEY NEVER CAME BACK.
pat
pat

HER HEART WAS SO BROKEN THAT SHE SURRENDERED TO THE ALIENS AND JOINED THEIR CAUSE.

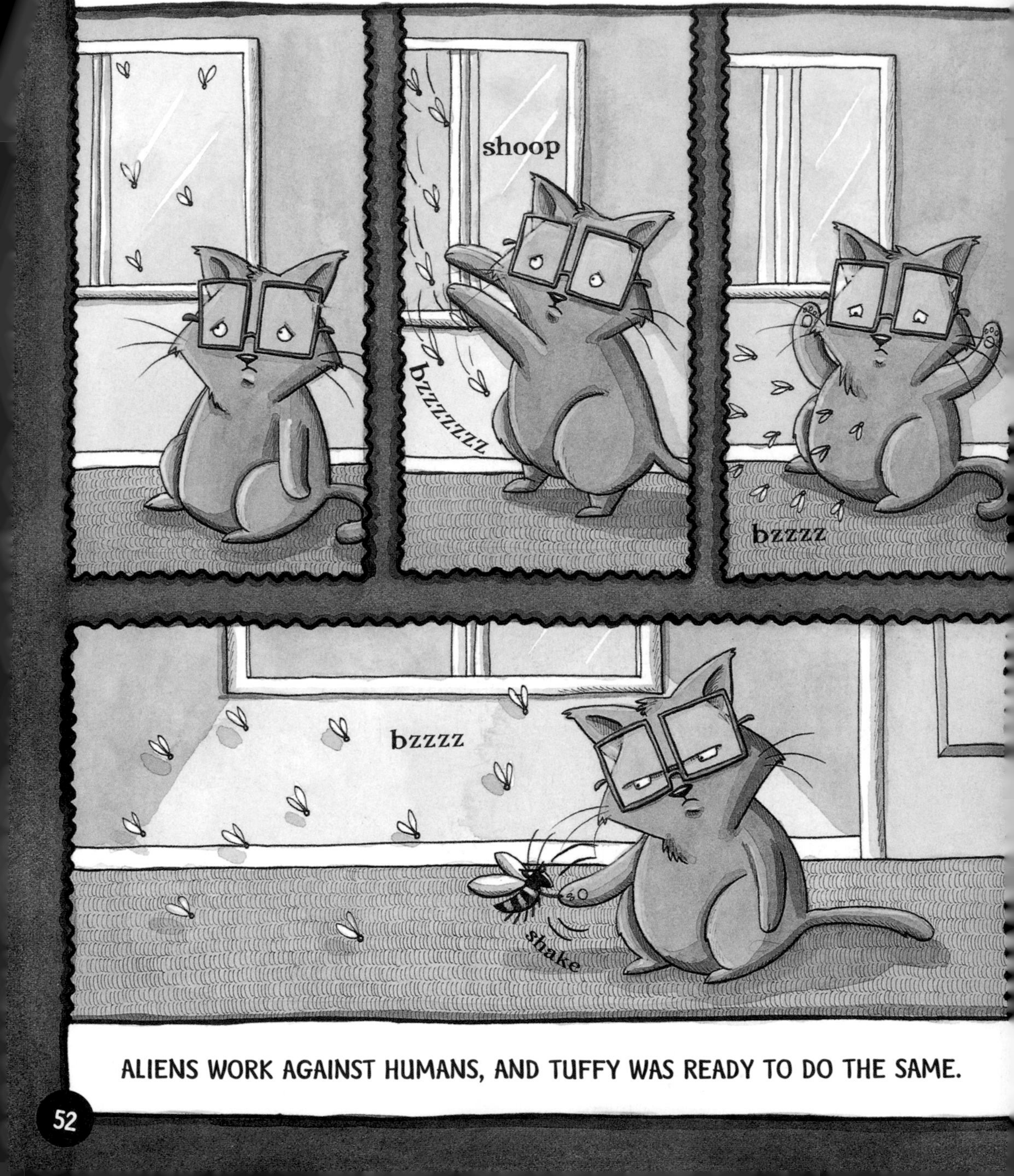
shoop
bzzzzzzz
bzzzz
bzzzz
shake

ALIENS WORK AGAINST HUMANS, AND TUFFY WAS READY TO DO THE SAME.

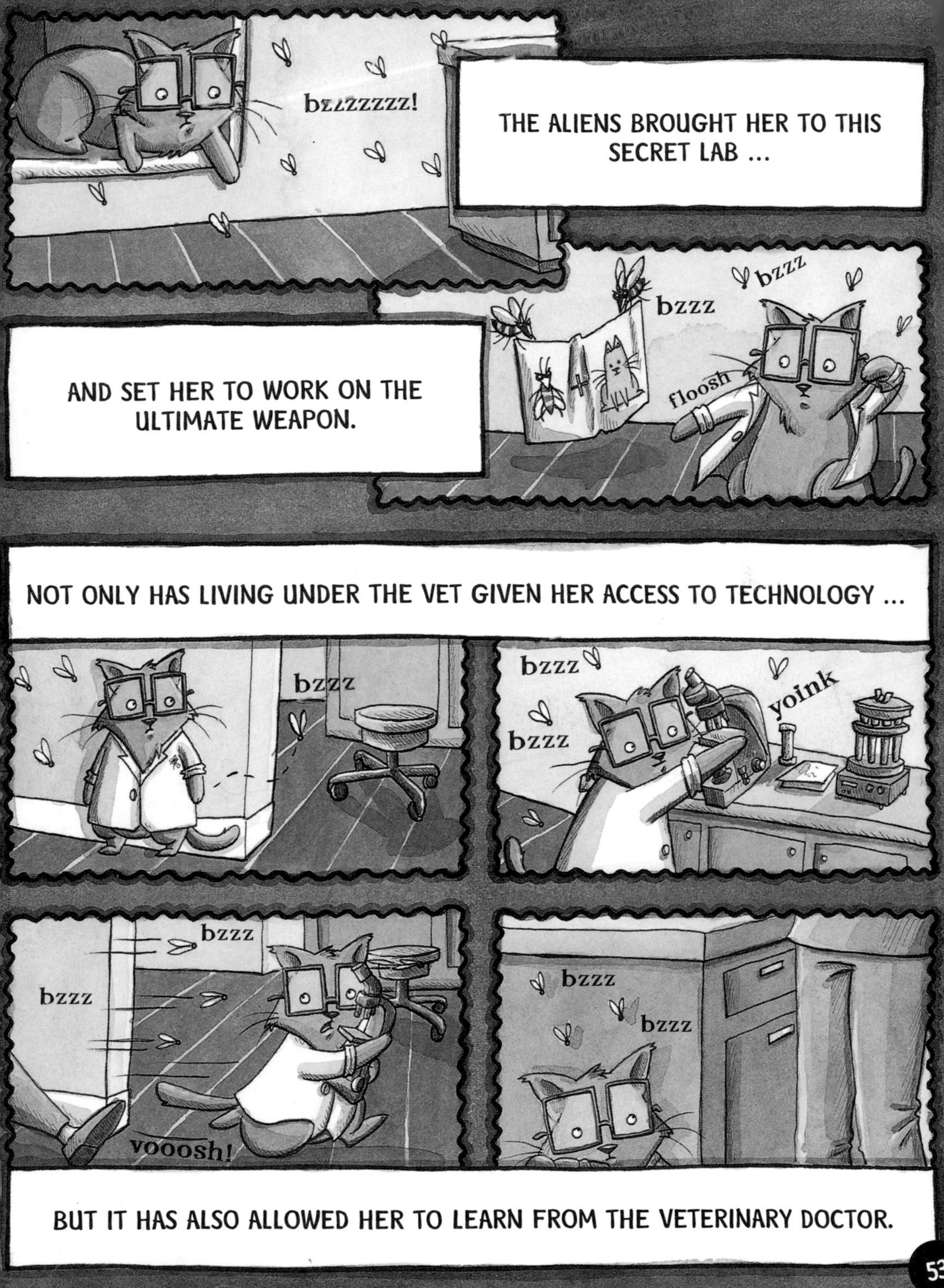
bzzzzzzz!
THE ALIENS BROUGHT HER TO THIS SECRET LAB ...
AND SET HER TO WORK ON THE ULTIMATE WEAPON.
bzzz
bzzz
floosh
NOT ONLY HAS LIVING UNDER THE VET GIVEN HER ACCESS TO TECHNOLOGY ...
bzzz
bzzz
bzzz
yoink
bzzz
bzzz
vooosh!
bzzz
bzzz
BUT IT HAS ALSO ALLOWED HER TO LEARN FROM THE VETERINARY DOCTOR.

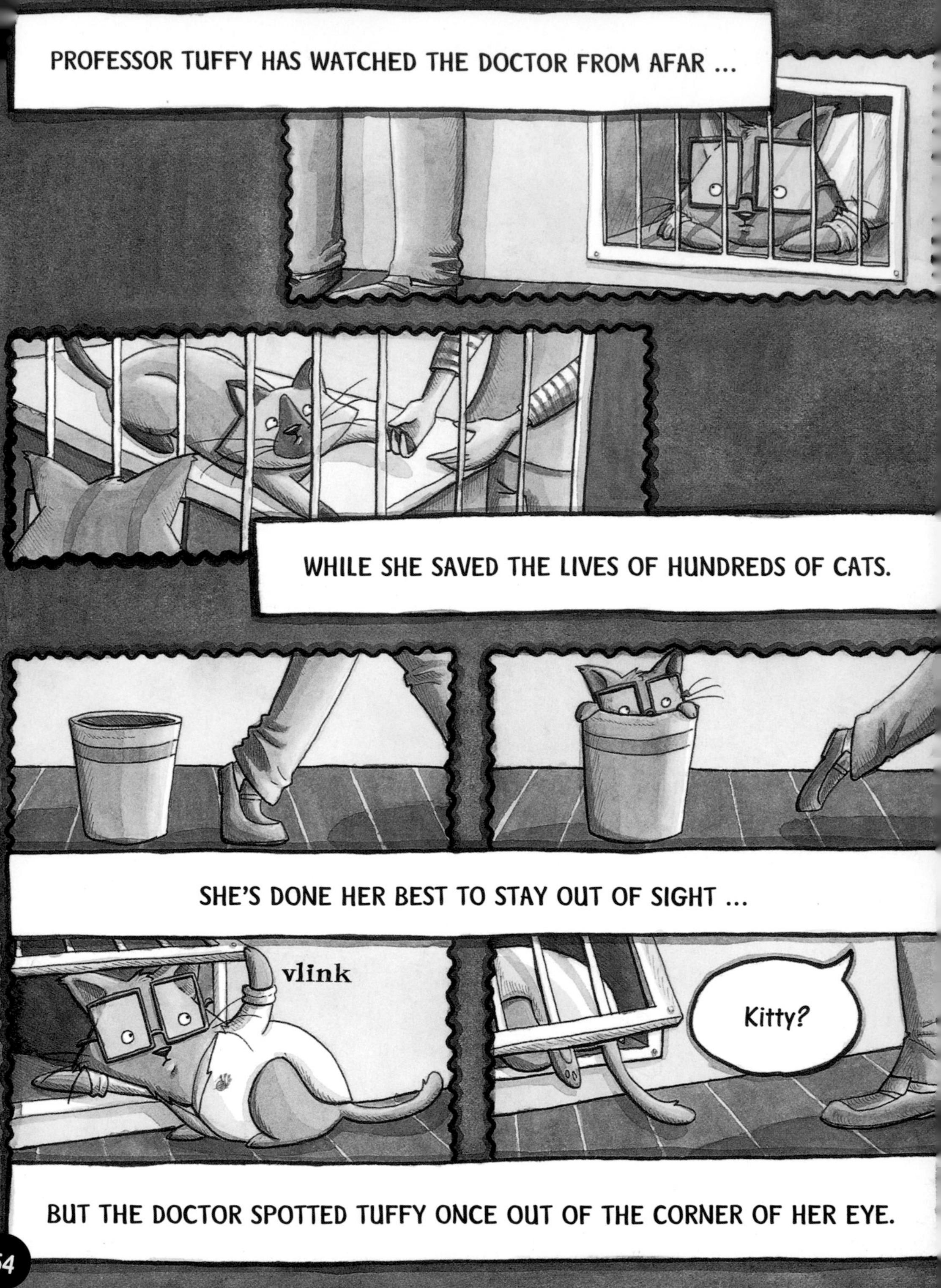
PROFESSOR TUFFY HAS WATCHED THE DOCTOR FROM AFAR ...
WHILE SHE SAVED THE LIVES OF HUNDREDS OF CATS.
SHE'S DONE HER BEST TO STAY OUT OF SIGHT ...
vlink
Kitty?
BUT THE DOCTOR SPOTTED TUFFY ONCE OUT OF THE CORNER OF HER EYE.

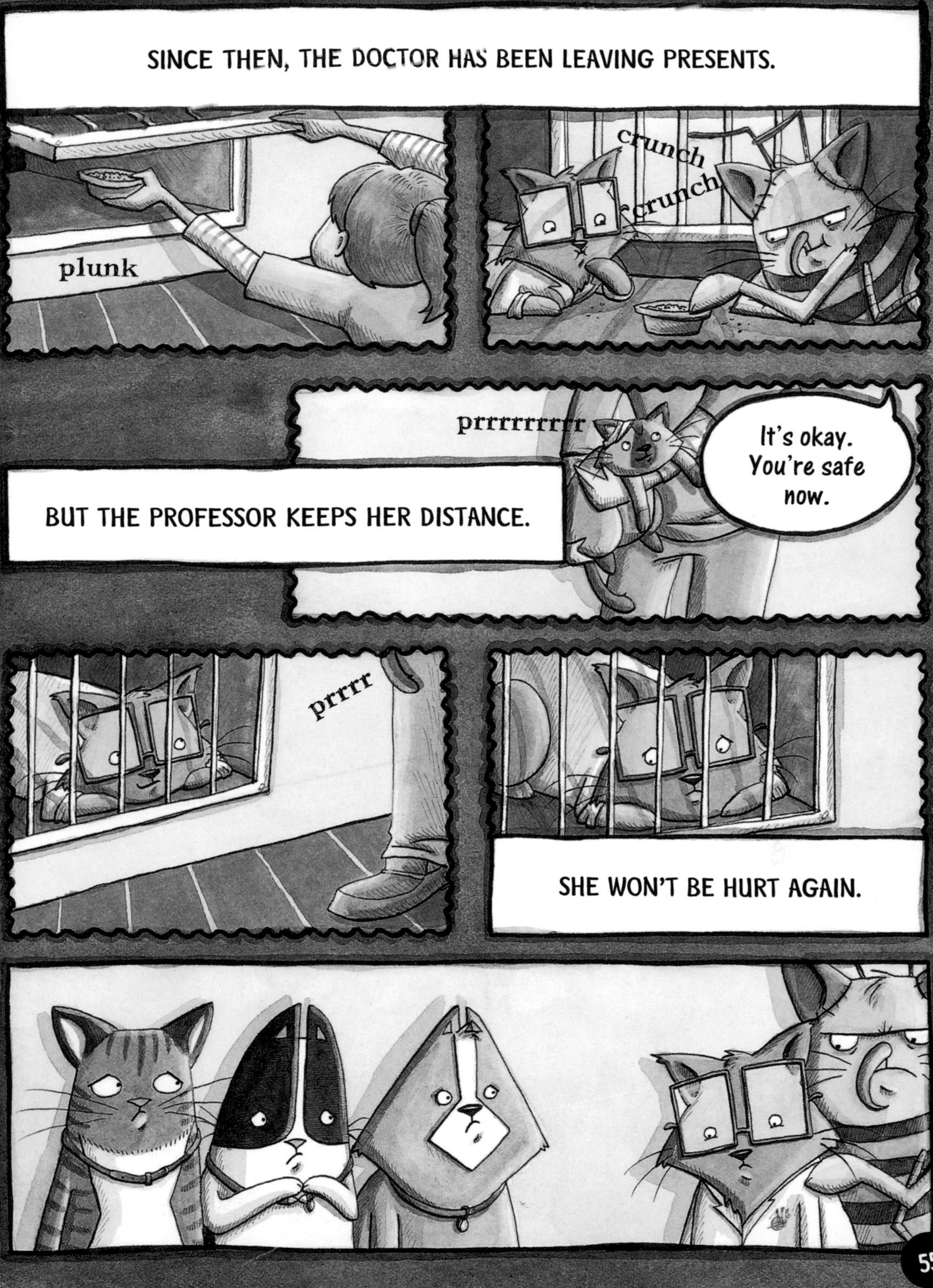
SINCE THEN, THE DOCTOR HAS BEEN LEAVING PRESENTS.
plunk
crunch
crunch
prrrrrrrrr
It's okay. You're safe now.
BUT THE PROFESSOR KEEPS HER DISTANCE.
prrrr
SHE WON'T BE HURT AGAIN.

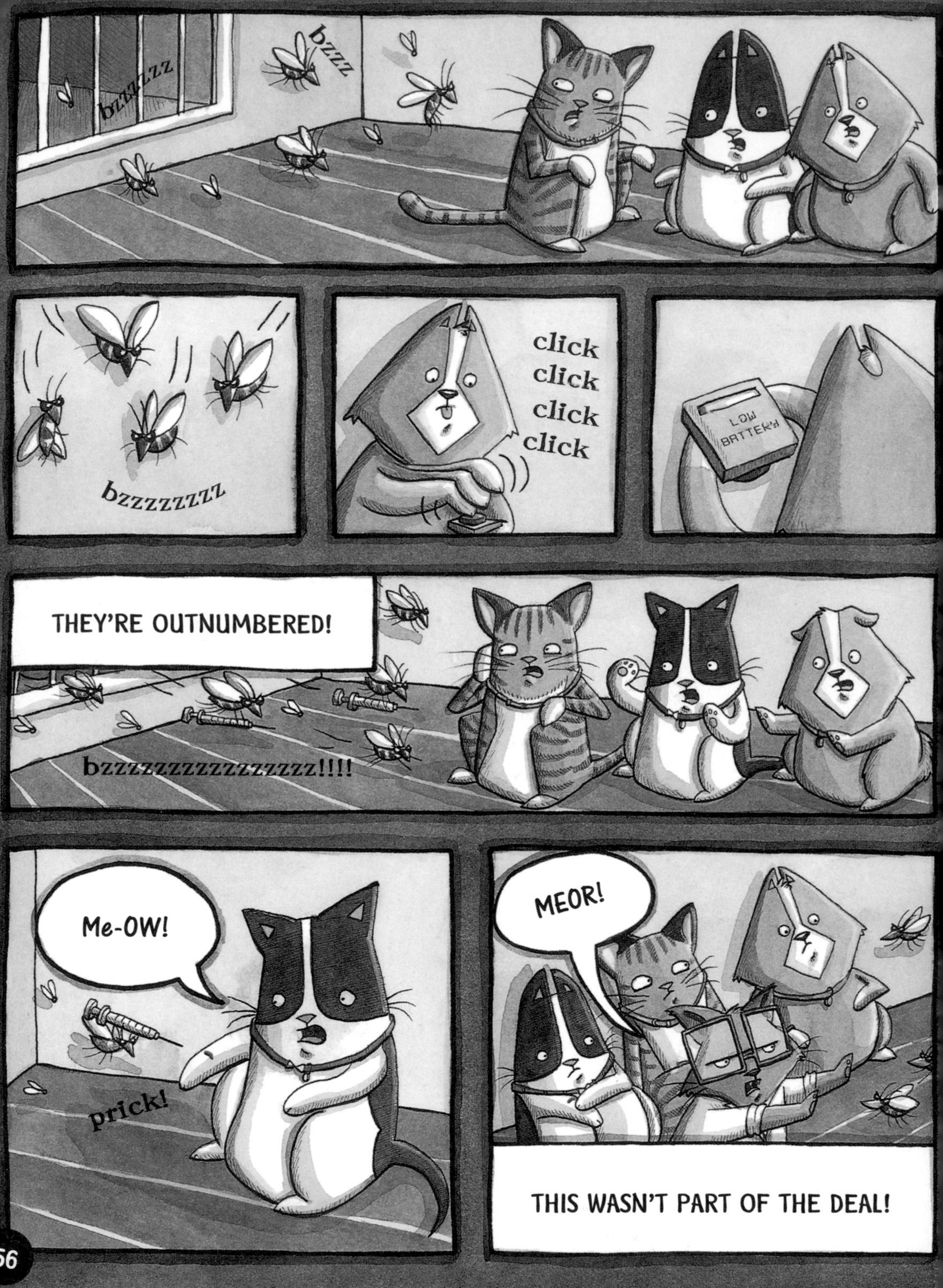

bzzzzzz
bzzz
bzzzzzzz
click
click
click
click
LOW BATTERY
THEY'RE OUTNUMBERED!
bzzzzzzzzzzzzzzzz!!!!
Me-OW!
prick!
MEOR!
THIS WASN'T PART OF THE DEAL!

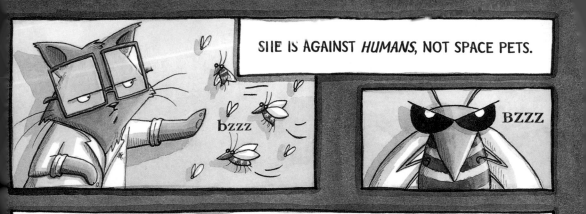

SHE IS AGAINST *HUMANS*, NOT SPACE PETS.
bzzz
BZZZ
THE ALIENS HAVE WHAT THEY WANTED. THEY DON'T NEED HER ANYMORE.
MEOOOR?!?
bzzz
bzzz
bzzz
HOW COULD THIS HAPPEN? TUFFY HAS BEEN BETRAYED AGAIN!
bzzz
bzzz
bzzz
POW!
CRUNCH!

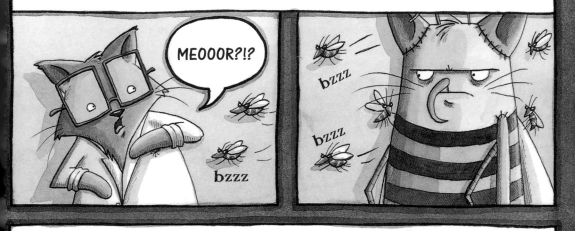

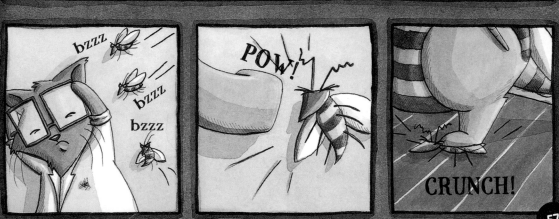

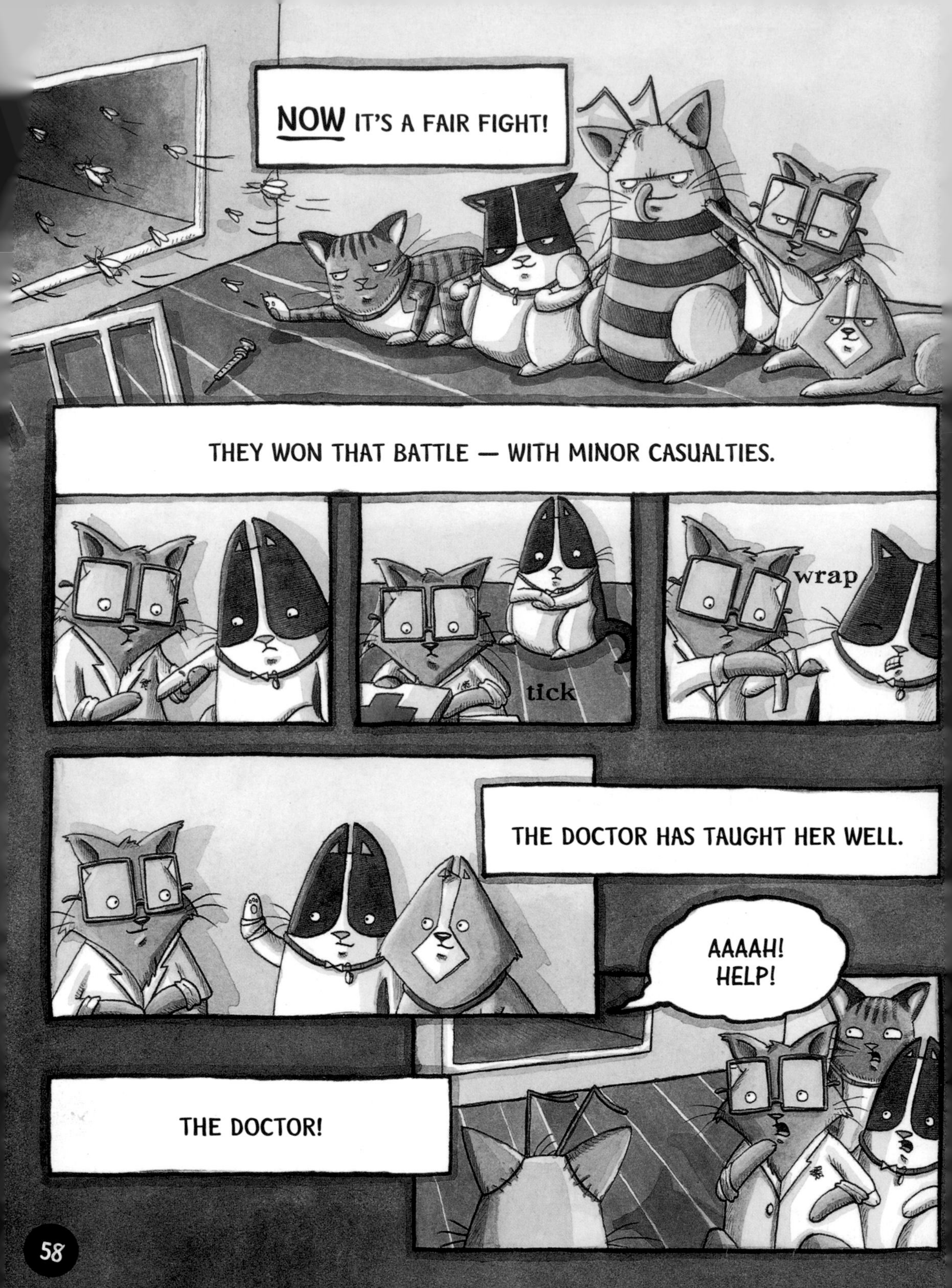
NOW IT'S A FAIR FIGHT!
THEY WON THAT BATTLE — WITH MINOR CASUALTIES.
tick
wrap
THE DOCTOR HAS TAUGHT HER WELL.
AAAAH! HELP!
THE DOCTOR!

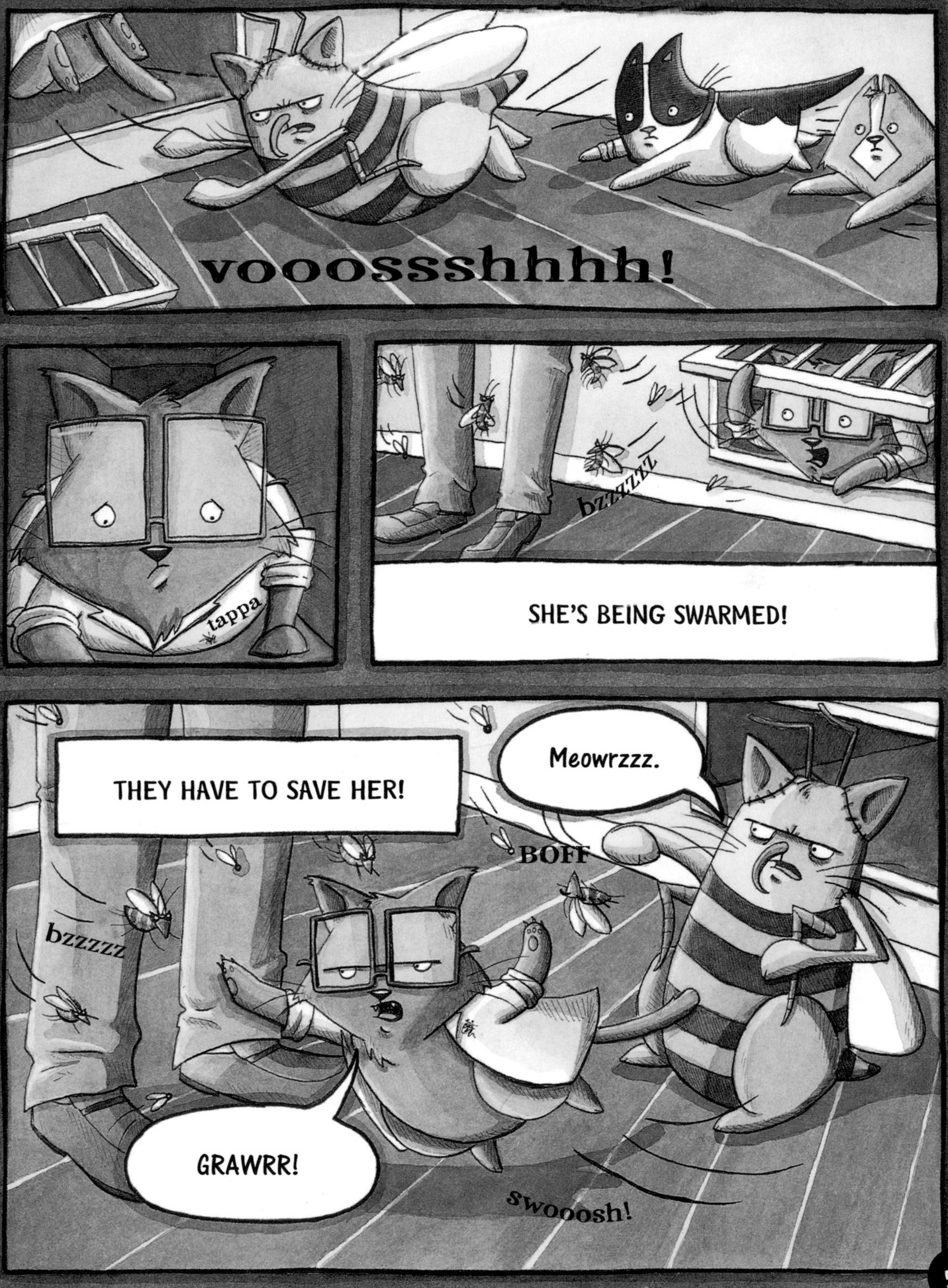
voooosshhhh!
tappa
bzzzzzz
SHE'S BEING SWARMED!
THEY HAVE TO SAVE HER!
Meowrzzz.
BOFF
bzzzzz
GRAWRR!
swooosh!

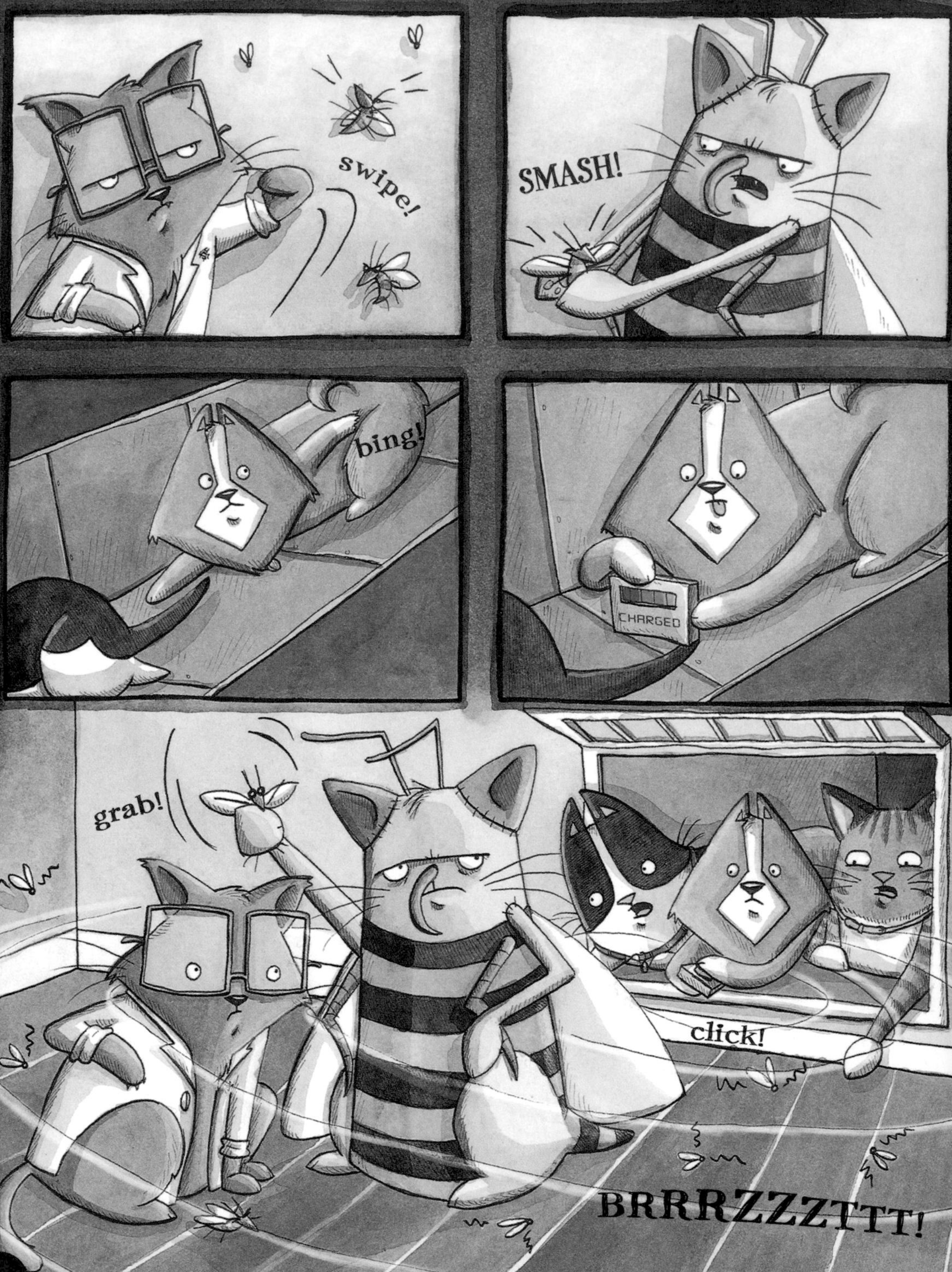
swipe!
SMASH!
bing!
CHARGED
grab!
click!
BRRRZZZTTT!

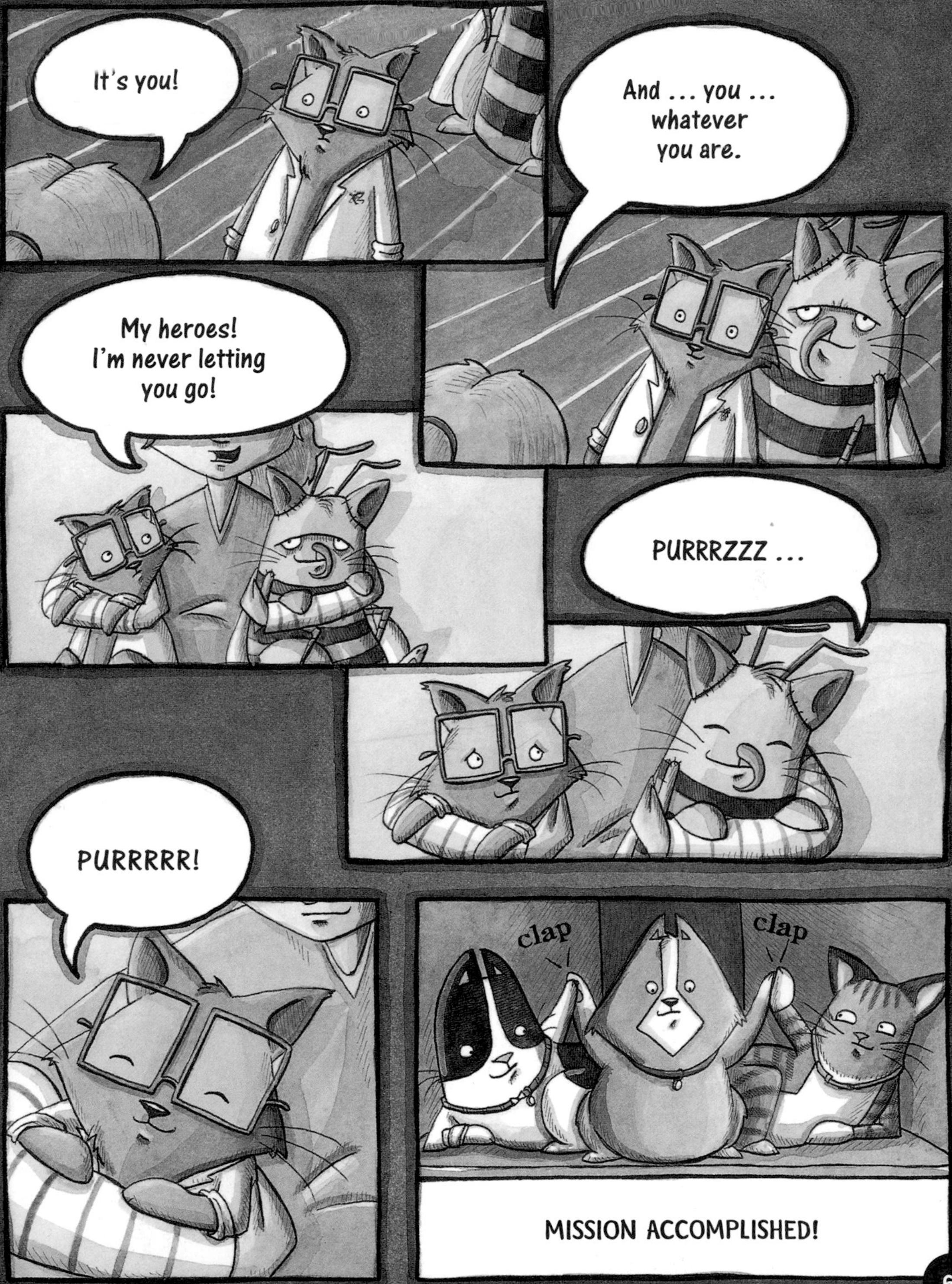
It's you!
And . . . you . . . whatever you are.
My heroes! I'm never letting you go!
PURRRZZZ . . .
PURRRRR!
clap
clap
MISSION ACCOMPLISHED!

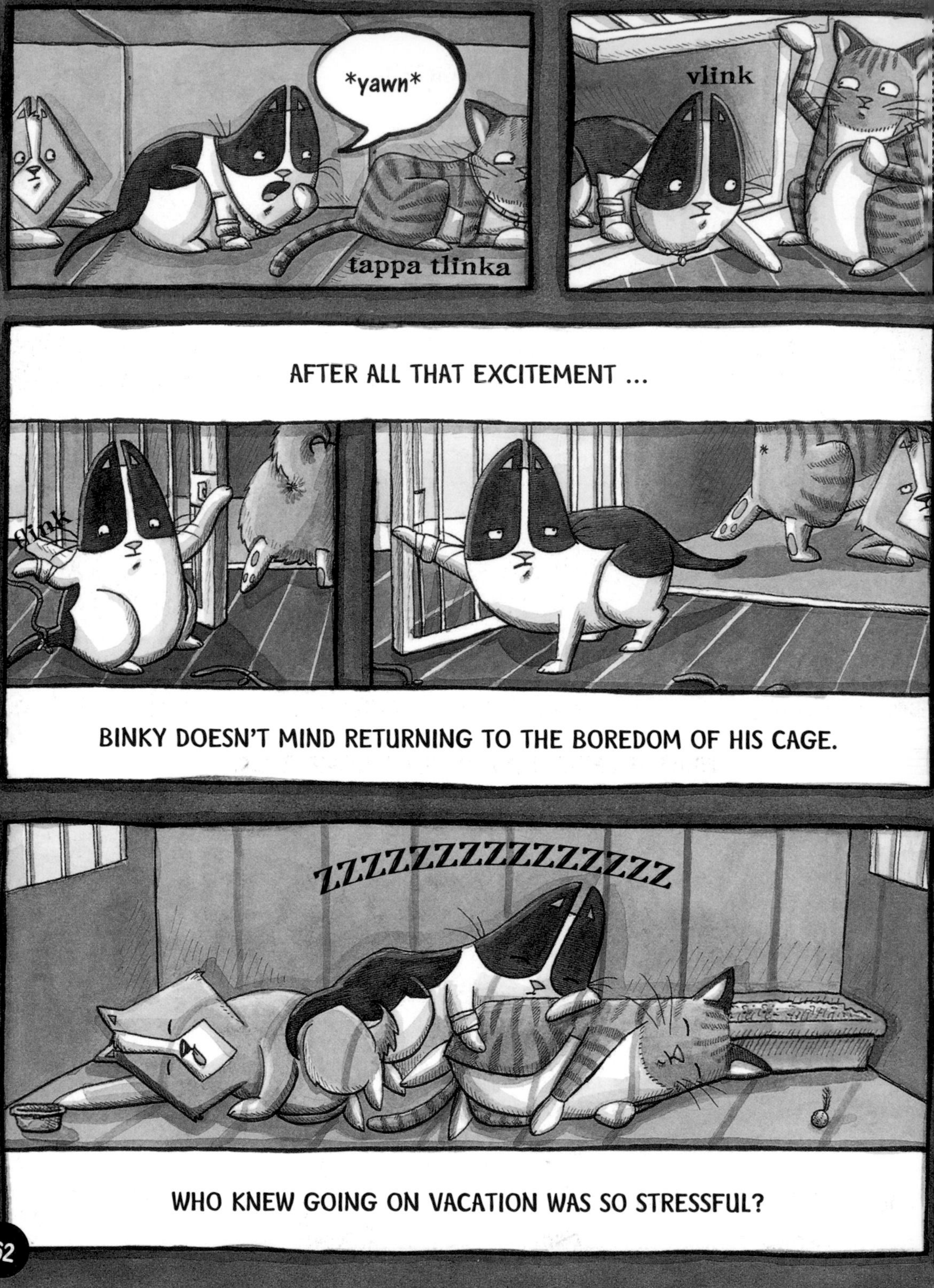
yawn
tappa tlinka
vlink
AFTER ALL THAT EXCITEMENT ...
tink
BINKY DOESN'T MIND RETURNING TO THE BOREDOM OF HIS CAGE.
ZZZZZZZZZZZZZZZZZ
WHO KNEW GOING ON VACATION WAS SO STRESSFUL?

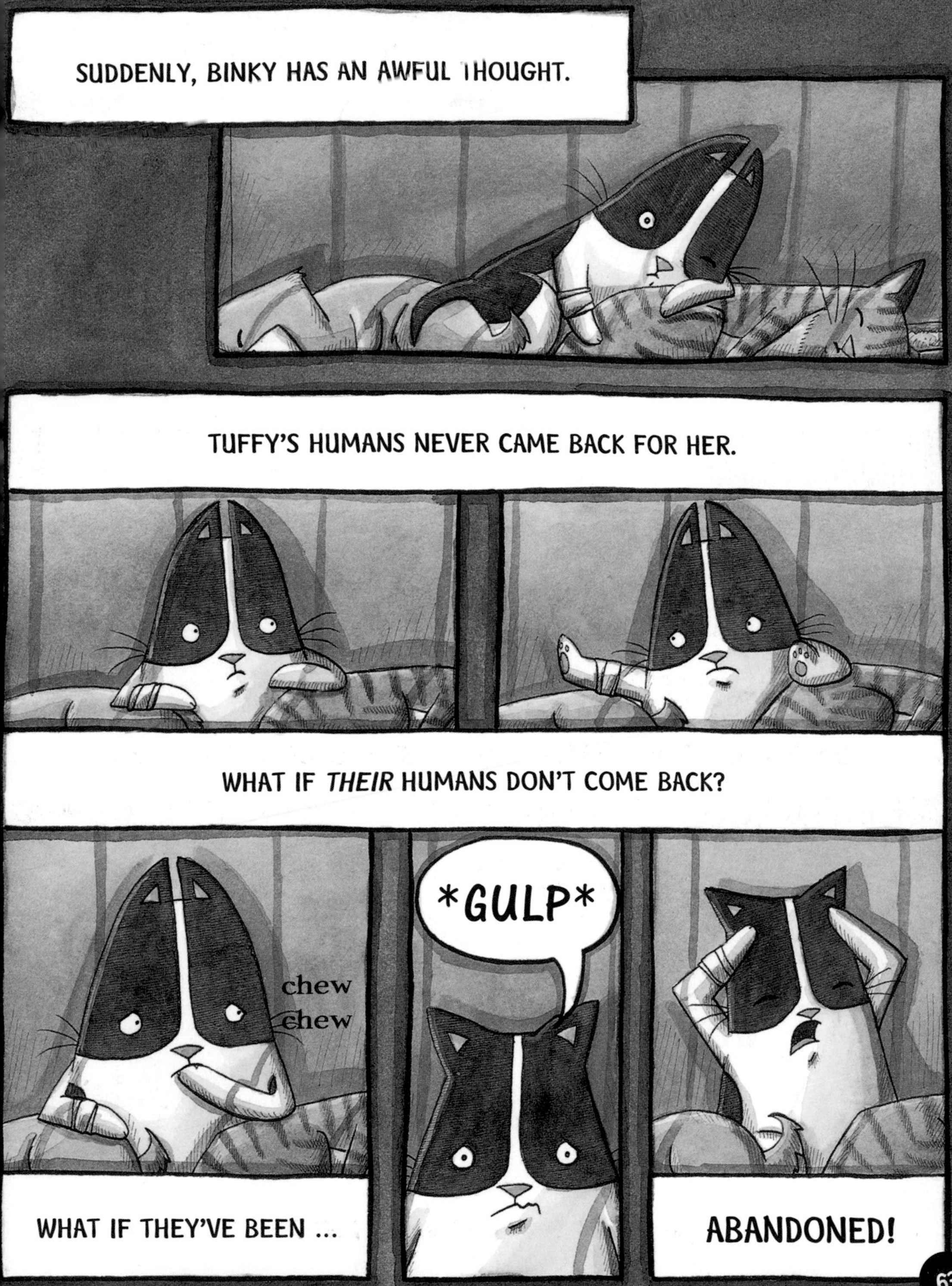
SUDDENLY, BINKY HAS AN AWFUL THOUGHT.
TUFFY'S HUMANS NEVER CAME BACK FOR HER.
WHAT IF *THEIR* HUMANS DON'T COME BACK?
chew
chew
WHAT IF THEY'VE BEEN ...
GULP
ABANDONED!

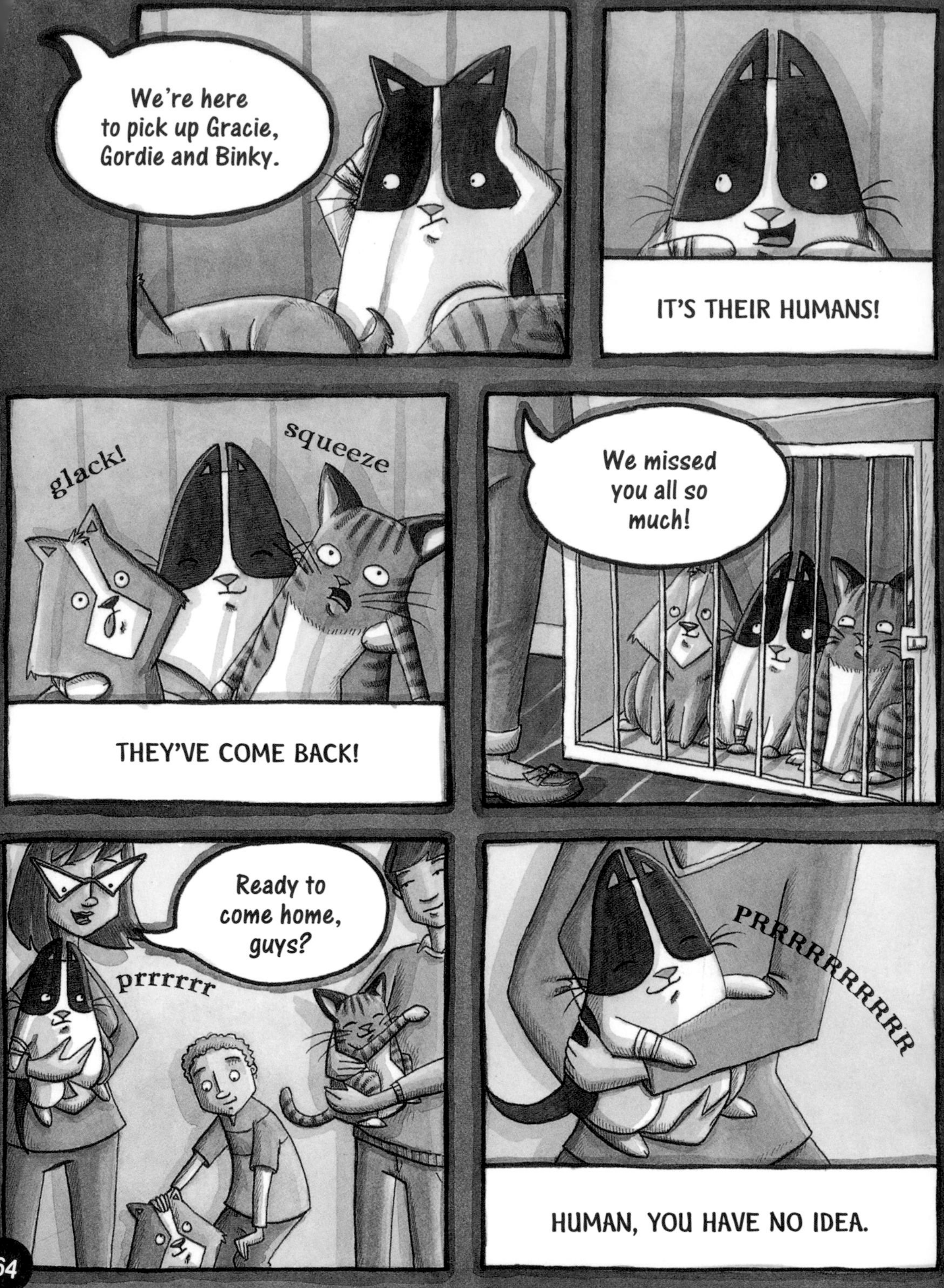
We're here to pick up Gracie, Gordie and Binky.
IT'S THEIR HUMANS!
glack!
squeeze
THEY'VE COME BACK!
We missed you all so much!
Ready to come home, guys?
prrrrrr
PRRRRRRRRRRR
HUMAN, YOU HAVE NO IDEA.